SUNNY SWEET
Can SO Get Lost

Sunny Sweet
Can SO Get Lost

Jennifer Ann Mann

illustrated by Jana Christy

BLOOMSBURY
NEW YORK   LONDON   NEW DELHI   SYDNEY

To my Mann, Kevin

Text copyright © 2015 by Jennifer Ann Mann
Illustrations copyright © 2015 by Jana Christy
All rights reserved. No part of this book may be reproduced or transmitted in any form
or by any means, electronic or mechanical, including photocopying, recording, or by any
information storage and retrieval system, without permission in writing from the publisher.

First published in the United States of America in February 2015
by Bloomsbury Children's Books
www.bloomsbury.com

Bloomsbury is a registered trademark of Bloomsbury Publishing Plc

For information about permission to reproduce selections from this book, write to
Permissions, Bloomsbury Children's Books, 1385 Broadway, New York, NY 10018
Bloomsbury books may be purchased for business or promotional use. For information on
bulk purchases please contact Macmillan Corporate and Premium Sales Department at
specialmarkets@macmillan.com

Library of Congress Cataloging-in-Publication Data
Mann, Jennifer Ann.
Sunny Sweet can so get lost / by Jennifer Ann Mann.
pages   cm
Summary: Eleven-year-old Masha has looked forward to spending summer vacation with
her father at a South Dakota dude ranch, but her "evil genius" little sister, Sunny, arranges
for them to go to a mathematics camp in Maine, instead.
ISBN 978-1-61963-505-0 (hardcover) • ISBN 978-1-61963-506-7 (e-book)
[1. Sisters—Fiction. 2. Genius—Fiction. 3. Lost children—Fiction. 4. Camps—Fiction.
5. Adventure and adventurers—Fiction.] I. Title.
PZ7.M31433Sl 2015   [Fic]—dc23   2014009084

Book design by John Candell
Typeset by Westchester Book Composition
Printed and bound in the U.S.A. by Thomson-Shore Inc., Dexter, Michigan
2 4 6 8 10 9 7 5 3 1

All papers used by Bloomsbury Publishing, Inc., are natural, recyclable products
made from wood grown in well-managed forests. The manufacturing processes
conform to the environmental regulations of the country of origin.

Sunny Sweet Can So Get Lost

You smell like a pickle."

"Yeah, I know," I said.

The little kid standing in front of me at the airport was not the first person to notice. It had been two months since my little sister had exploded red dye all over me in the name of science and I *still* smelled like vinegar! Actually, I smelled like twenty-two bottles of vinegar because that is what it took to remove my evil little sister's latest science experiment from my skin.

"I like pickles," said the little kid, licking his lips.

"I'm not a pickle."

My mother had filled our bathtub up with vinegar, and I had soaked in it for four straight hours. So maybe I was a pickle. I pulled my phone closer to my face to block the kid from my sight.

The kid didn't move.

"It's vinegar you smell," Sunny said, looking up from her book. "Vinegar is a liquid used in the process of preserving food, like cucumbers, which when preserved in vinegar are called pickles. This is why you think that my sister, Masha, smells like one."

The kid blinked at Sunny for a half second and then took off—hopping back to his mother along a row of attached chairs.

"Did you know . . . ," Sunny started.

"No," I said.

This didn't stop her. It never did. ". . . that the word 'vinegar' comes from the Anglo-French words '*vin egre,*' which mean sour wine? So what you really smell like is sour wine."

"Can't you just let me smell like a pickle?" I asked.

My phone rang, and I clicked it on. "Hi, Mom!"

"Hey, Masha. Are you and Sunny in Boston?"

"Yeah, we're here."

"Is the unaccompanied minor attendant with you?"

"Yes, Mom, I'm looking right at her and she's looking right back at me. Her name is Wendi, with an *i*. And no you cannot talk to her. Sunny and I are fine."

"I wasn't even going to ask." She laughed. But I knew that she was. My mom was pretty nervous about Sunny and me flying out alone to meet our dad for summer vacation. We had to fly from Newark Airport in New Jersey up to Boston in Massachusetts. And from there, we'd fly all the way out west to South Dakota. My mom needed to fly to Russia to be with my grandmother for a surgery, so my father surprised Sunny and me with a trip to the Lone Creek Dude Ranch.

Sunny and I hadn't seen our dad since Christmas. But any butterflies swirling around my belly about not seeing him for so long were pretty much buried alive by the *awesometastic* news that I was going to get to ride a horse! My father sent us the brochure in the mail. On the cover was a shiny black horse running across a prairie. I made my mom rent *Black Beauty* that night, and I'd watched it every day since . . . twice a day on Sundays.

"I'm boarding soon," Mom said. She was still back in Newark Airport, where we'd left her that morning. "Let me say a quick hi to your sister."

I tried to hand Sunny my phone. She wouldn't take it. Instead, she put both her hands to her throat and pretended she couldn't speak. I rolled my eyes. "Sorry, Mom, she can't talk. She's got laryngitis."

My mom snorted with laugher. The little genius's new project these days was to follow my mother around as her mini personal secretary, writing her e-mails and picking up her phone calls. Whenever Sunny answered a marketing call, she would tell them that my mom had laryngitis and couldn't talk. My mom thought it was the funniest thing ever, especially when Sunny explained how the larynx and trachea worked to the poor marketing people.

"Well, tell your sister I love her. And that I love the group texts you guys are sending to my e-mail. They are so cute."

"Group texts?" I repeated, glancing over at Sunny. Sunny didn't take her eyes from her book, but I could tell by how she stared at one spot on the page that she heard me.

"That reminds me," she continued. "I got the strangest e-mail from your father."

"An e-mail from Dad? What did he say?" I asked. "Was it about my horse?"

Sunny put her book down and swiped at my phone. I batted her off like a fly.

"Masha Sweet," my mother said, sighing. When my mom calls me this, I know she's serious. And she had been calling me this a lot in the last few weeks. "Your father is not buying you a horse. I know that he said that he had a surprise for you and Sunny, but I'm sure the surprise is *not a horse*. I wish you would stop hoping because you're just going to be disappointed."

"Well, what exactly did he say?" I moaned. I wasn't going to stop hoping for my horse. Hope was all I had. Anyway, what else could the surprise be? He was taking us to a dude ranch, and he had made a big deal of having a surprise for me and Sunny. I didn't see how my mom could think that I *wasn't* getting a horse!

Sunny tried to snatch the phone from me again. I swooped away from her and into the seat on the other side of me. Unfortunately, that seat happened to be occupied by a man reading a newspaper. The man cleared his throat, warning me, I guess, to calm down.

I smiled, thinking about how the man had just treated me like a normal kid, using a normal way that adults do to signal kids to cut it out. And this is because, except for smelling slightly like a garden salad, I *was* a normal kid. It hadn't been that long ago that Sunny had glued a million plastic flowers to my head and I had to have my head shaved. Or that I had been covered in red dye when Sunny had exploded a bottle of ketchup all over me so she could win a science fair. But today my hair was looking pretty cute in a bob. And today my skin was splotch-free. In fact, today dinky Dr. Frankenstein had not done one terrible thing to me.

I felt a tiny pinch in my stomach at that last thought. I looked over at Sunny. She was busy with her phone.

"Oh, I'm boarding," my mom said, breathless. She always got so excited when it was time to get on a plane. A big wave of missing her broke over me. She was getting on a plane and we were getting on a plane, but we weren't getting on a plane together.

"Kisses and hugs," she said. "I'll give Babushka all your love, and you guys have a great time with your father. Tell Sunny the same. Oh, and tell her that I loved finding her travel safety plan in my carry-on." She gave a tiny shriek of joy. "The organization chart of emergency numbers and addresses was terrific! And the detailed outline of contingency emergency plans for natural disasters and power outages was really above and beyond, even for your little sister."

Again I looked over at Sunny. She was still playing with her phone. I didn't like hearing about this stuff . . . the safety plan and the texts. That pinch in my stomach was growing into an actual ache. Sunny was up to something. I looked around. Everything looked okay. We were at our gate. Wendi with an *i* was constantly staring over at us from the ticket counter as if we might disappear at any moment. I had my ticket information and ID around my neck. Sunny had hers. I just wish my mom hadn't said that thing about Sunny because one thing I knew to be true . . . *nothing was above and beyond my little sister.*

"A gazillion kisses right back, Mom. I love you, love you, love you," I told her.

She smacked me a real kiss through the phone and then she was gone. I took a deep breath filled with wishing that my mother were here with us or that we were there with her. No . . . wait. I didn't want to be going to Russia to watch my grandmother's hip get fixed—I wanted to be going to the Lone Creek Dude Ranch to ride horses!

The sight of Sunny's skinny little fingers bouncing about on her phone keys caught my attention. "What are you doing?" I asked.

"What?"

"What are you doing?"

I looked closer at her phone. "Are you checking Mom's e-mails?" My heart fluttered. "Check the one from Dad. See if he said anything about my horse."

"I hate horses," she said, not taking her eyes off her screen.

I leaned back in my airport chair and closed my eyes. *I love horses.*

The vision of my horse shimmered into my head. He was a dark chocolate brown with a long black mane. His eyes were huge and kind. His coat shone from all of my brushing. We walked together, his nose nuzzling my ear. And then I jumped onto his back and we rode along cliffs overlooking the ocean.

Wendi with an *i* interrupted my dream.

"You're going to be boarding soon," she said, and then I watched as she turned and walked back over to the tiny ticket counter to chat with the flight attendants at the entrance to the gate. Over the counter in dotted red lit-up letters it said PORTLAND.

"Hey, Sunny, I remember Mom saying that the airport we were flying into was like Sioux Falls or something," I said, pointing at the sign.

Sunny glanced up at the sign. Then she hopped out of her seat. "I have to go to the bathroom."

"You just went."

"Um," she said. "I have to go again."

I didn't want to go to the bathroom again. I wanted to go back to dreaming my wonderful horse dreams. We weren't supposed to go anywhere alone, even the bathroom. So if I called Wendi with an *i,* I would have to go too. I looked up at Wendi with an *i*. She was bent over the desk writing something. "Just go," I said. "But hurry up."

I immediately went back to dreaming about Oscar or Charlie, which both sounded like solid horse names. But I also kind of liked the more horsey-sounding names, like Thunder and Black Cloud. I got my phone back out and went to this website I'd found with a ton of pictures of horses and started scrolling through them—white horses, brown horses, white-and-brown horses, horses running in groups, horses running through long grass, horses jumping, horses with giant hooves, horses pulling carts, horses, horses, horses . . .

The quietness poked at me. I looked up to see the last few people at the gate heading onto the plane.

"Sunny?" I looked around me. "Sunny!" I yelped.

I jumped out of my seat. Where was Sunny? Where was Wendi with an *i*? How long had I been looking at horses? I ran down the wide airport hall and into the bathroom. "Sunny!" I called. There was no answer, but I did hear something . . . It was Sunny's voice in my head . . . *I hate horses.*

All of a sudden an avalanche of things Sunny had been doing and saying lately rolled over me—Sunny asking over and over why we couldn't just go to our old house in Pennsylvania to see Dad, or Sunny begging to go with my mom to Babushka's in Saint Petersburg. And then there was all her complaining about the dude ranch and how she didn't like square dancing and how they would probably only be serving ribs, which she couldn't eat because my six-year-old sister had become a vegetarian. Finally, in my head I heard her say, "I have to go to the bathroom," and I knew . . . *She didn't really have to go to the bathroom.*

HOLY FROZEN RAVIOLI . . . Sunny Sweet was gone!

I gave a short little howl and ran out of the bathroom and straight into Wendi with an *i*.

"Oh my gosh!" Wendi with an *i* cried, almost hugging me. "Where have you been?"

"Uh . . . uh," I said.

She locked arms with me and pulled me toward the gate. I stumbled along next to her, searching every face in the airport for Sunny's.

"My sister," I huffed, "is los—" I stopped. Sunny Sweet was gone, but she wasn't lost. Sunny Sweet didn't get lost. You had to *not* know where you were to be lost, and wherever Sunny was at this moment, she knew exactly where she was! I thought about what my mother said on the phone, about some sort of group text that Sunny sent. And that safety thing that she put in my mom's bag. Then I thought about Sunny taking all of my mom's phone calls and writing all her e-mails for the last couple of months. I didn't know the reason why she was doing these things, but I did know that there was a reason. She was definitely up to something. And this time, I wasn't going to be a part of it.

"Time to get on that plane," Wendi with an *i* said, pointing toward the flight attendant waiting at the gate.

I took one last look around. I bet Sunny was watching me right this minute. I bet she was wondering what I'd do next. I wasn't going to let her do this to me again. I thought about Oscar/Charlie/Thunder/Black Cloud. I wanted my horse. That decided it.

Sunny Sweet can so get lost! But I certainly wasn't getting lost with her!

I turned and walked down the tiny airplane hallway. I was free, free, free of Sunny Sweet forever . . . or for at least three weeks, which was good enough. Plus I'd have two whole seats on the plane so I could stretch out and eat and . . . what was I doing? *Sunny!*

I swung around. There stood Wendi with an *i* with her arms crossed in front of her blocking my path. "My little sister. She's . . ." That's when I heard Sunny's voice coming from behind me. "On the plane?" I finished. I turned and hurried through the spaceship-looking portal of the plane. There was Sunny Sweet, standing with the pilot and telling jokes.

"Why did the chicken cross the Möbius strip?" she said.

"Why?" laughed the pilot.

"To get to the same side."

They both cracked up laughing.

"Hey, Masha, get it?" she asked. "Because a Möbius strip only has one side."

"I get it," I sighed, even though I didn't get it. I never got it. Even when I thought I got it, I didn't get it. I thought Sunny Sweet was lost. She wasn't. I thought Sunny Sweet was up to something. But she wasn't. I guess my evil-genius little sister really did like explaining laryngitis to poor, unsuspecting marketers and making up organization charts and detailed safety plans.

"Hey, Sunny," the pilot said. He already knew her name. "Do you want to announce our departure?" He held out a walkie-talkie-looking thing to her.

"I'm going to the bathroom," I told Sunny. "Be in the aisle seat when I get back. It's my turn to sit by the window."

I trudged down the aisle trying to get a minute of my life without my little sister in it. Sunny's voice followed me the entire way. "Ladies and gentlemen, please take your seats as we get ready for departure," she said. "Please turn off all electronic devices, such as cell phones and computers."

I closed the bathroom door and quickly pulled out my phone. I had a text from my friend Junchao. She was spending her summer vacation at some horrible science camp, although she seemed pretty excited about it. Junchao knew I was going to a dude ranch, but I didn't tell her about Oscar/Charlie/Thunder/ Black Cloud because I didn't want to ruin her happiness about only getting to go to a lousy camp when I was getting a horse! Her text said:

Don't ride off into the sunset!

I texted back my usual.

Ho-ho-ho.

Junchao was as tiny as a mouse but had the biggest, Santa Claus–iest laugh you ever heard. Every time I heard it, I had to laugh too.

Sunny's voice blared through speakers in the bathroom, giving me the local time we'd be landing. Even in here I couldn't get away from her. Then I felt the plane lurch as it pulled away from the airport gate.

I quickly texted my friend Alice good-bye and told her to have a great time. She was taking a family trip to Florida. A foundation gave them the trip because of Alice's spina bifida. Usually Alice hated being treated differently because of her spine not working right and because she needed a wheelchair, but she got over it really quickly when the words "Disney World" got mentioned. I might have been totally green if I wasn't getting my very own HORSE!

Alice and I planned that once I got good at riding him, I'd teach her how. We figured we could probably get her tied to the saddle somehow to make it safe. Anyway, Oscar/Charlie/Thunder/Black Cloud was going to be so gentle and smart, he would just know how to be careful carrying Alice around.

"Preparing for takeoff . . ." came Sunny's voice again.

They had better not be letting Sunny Sweet fly this plane! I opened up the door and hurried back to our row. Sunny was sitting in the aisle seat. Thank goodness. I leaped over her to get to the window. I buckled up and looked out at the bustle of the airport tarmac. Time to chill out and dream about trotting and cantering and galloping. The plane turned and stopped. The engine fired up beneath us, and we began to pull down the runway. I was rushing toward my horse!

"Hello, this is your captain speaking," said a friendly voice over the intercom.

"That's Bob," Sunny said.

"Our time of departure is 6:32 p.m. Eastern Daylight Time. And we should be landing in Portland, Maine, just around 7:15 p.m."

Portland, Maine?

I looked over at Sunny. She stared down at the page in her book, but I knew she was seeing me seeing her.

"What did Bob mean by Portland, M . . ." I couldn't even finish the sentence because I finally got it. I got all of it. Playing secretary for my mom, faking laryngitis, sending group texts, and writing up emergency plans, I got it. Sunny Sweet was getting lost— and she was taking me with her! We were not on our way to the Lone Creek Dude Ranch.

"But the tickets? And Wendi with an *i*?" I whispered.

She put down her book and looked at me. "Good planning," she said.

Oscar/Charlie/Thunder/Black Cloud. NOOOOO!

I struggled to open my seat belt. I was getting out of here.

"Keep that buckled," a flight attendant hissed from a few seats away.

"I need to . . . !" I shouted.

"After takeoff," she said, not letting me finish. But it was too late, and I knew it.

The plane lifted off the ground and into the air. I fell back into my seat and watched with wide-open eyes as the world grew smaller and smaller beneath us.

"But why?" I asked. I could barely look at her.

Sunny pulled a brochure from her backpack and put it on my lap.

I looked down.

"Math camp?" I shouted over the engine of the plane.

"Yes!" Sunny giggled. "It's going to be so great. They have a whole series on robotics, and one on

INQUIRE
INVESTIGATE
INVENT

Blending Science, Technology, Engineering,
and Merriment since 1952.

**Welcome to The Newton
Camp of Mathematics!**

mechanical engineering, and one on environmental sustainability, and one on genetics . . ." She had to stop to breathe. "We will actually get to genetically modify cells to smell like other stuff, like flowers or rotten eggs or anything. And look!" she said, her little hands shaking with excitement as she opened the brochure on my lap and pointed at a heading.

I read:

FUN WITH DNA

"We're going to get to extract DNA from our very own cells!" She squealed, snatching the brochure from my lap and flipping through it. "Just think, Masha, space rovers and astrophysics and new geometric worlds and . . ."

"Horses," I choked. "What about horses?"

"Horses?" Sunny snorted—her nose now buried deep within the brochure. "I doubt it."

I started to feel woozy. I couldn't breathe. I needed air. I groped the seat around me.

"What are you doing?"

"What does it look like I'm doing?" I snapped. "I'm looking for an oxygen mask."

"Why?" she asked. "The aircraft's pressurization is fine. Look at this." She poked the brochure back in my face. "We gather our DNA by spitting into a cup."

I shoved the brochure away from me and pressed my entire body against the window of the plane to get as far away from Sunny Sweet as I could. We were passing through a bunch of fluffy white clouds. *How could she do this?*

"I'm calling Mom as soon as we land," I said. I felt as if I might throw up.

"A typical commercial flight between New York and Saint Petersburg, Russia, is approximately nine hours and five minutes," she said. "But of course, the exact time depends on wind speeds."

"Then I'm calling Dad."

"He went to Thailand," she said.

"What do you mean he went to Thailand?" I put my head in my hands and groaned. I was definitely going to throw up. "It's really over. We're really lost."

"Not all those who wander are lost," Sunny said, flipping through her dumb brochure. "That's a quote from J. R. R. Tolkien. He wrote *The Lord of the Rings*."

"Here's a quote for you," I said. " 'Annoying little sisters who wander often get lost when they are shoved into very deep wells.' Masha Sweet wrote that." I smiled.

Ho-Ho-Ho

Compliments of the captain," said the flight attendant as she handed Sunny and me red fizzy drinks with a ton of cherries in them.

"Cool," chirped Sunny.

I wanted to wave mine away on account of my life being over so why bother drinking a red fizzy drink, but the cherries were the kind that had been living in sugary syrup. And I love those. I sipped on my drink and wondered how I would get us out of this one. There was no bus to sneak onto this time like we did after Sunny glued those flowers to my head. And

I couldn't just call Alice and have her think up a good idea like pretending I was an artist that time Sunny exploded red dye all over me. Although I knew that if I did call Alice she would come up with something. I pulled out my journal and turned to the back page and wrote *How to get home?* at the top.

"What are you doing?" asked Sunny, trying to peek at what I'd written.

"Nothing," I snapped.

It was going to be a very long time before I forgave Sunny Sweet for this one. I pictured Sunny and me as little old ladies hobbling about on our canes. And then I pictured me whacking her over the head with mine. My little sister had really done it this time.

Sunny read the words from my journal page out loud. "How to get home?" She made it sound like I was the one in first grade and not her.

She looked up at me. "Did you know that you're using the scientific method to solve your problem?" she asked.

I ignored her.

"The first step in the scientific method is to ask a

question," she continued, pointing down at the page in my journal. "You're really going to love Camp Newton, Masha."

I glared at her. And then I wrote, *1. Call Alice.* Just writing these two words made me feel better. I looked out the window at the passing sky and sighed. When we land, I'll call Alice. She'll know what to do. Then it struck me . . . *when we land!* What will happen when we land? There will be another Wendi with an *i.* Maybe she'd be Amee with an *ee* or Tyna with a *y,* but no matter what weird way she spelled her name, she would exist. I'd finally found a flaw in skinny little Lord Voldemort's plan!

"Sunny," I said, turning to my little sister. "You know that there will be someone assigned to us when we land. And when that person finds out that there is no one picking us up at the airport, she's going to freak. And then your whole entire plan will crumble into dust."

Sunny sucked the last of her fizzy drink out of her cup with a loud slurp. "Someone is picking us up."

"Who?"

"Dr. Singh."

"Who?"

"Dr. Singh. She's a theoretical quantum physicist and the director of Camp Newton."

"How do you know?"

"I've been reading all about her work on wave particles. Only a quantum physicist would be studying wave particles."

"No," I said. "Not how do you know she's a theater quack fuzziest, or whatever you just said, but how do you know she's picking us up?"

"Because I've been e-mailing her. Or, I mean," she giggled, "Mom has."

"Arghhh," I wailed, throwing myself against the back of my seat. "How could you do this to us?"

"It was easy," she said. "Mommy gave me her credit card to book the flights. You know how she can never navigate those kinds of websites. I booked the tickets online and just put in the information to fly us from Boston to Portland, Maine, instead of to South Dakota. When I showed Mommy the tickets, she saw that we were flying to Boston right on top. Before she could look more, I put the tickets into the travel packet

I created and asked her not to mess up my organization. Mommy *loves* it when I organize for her. She didn't touch a thing. Then I e-mailed Daddy like I was Mommy, and told him there was a change in plans."

"So you lied!" I snarled.

"No I didn't," Sunny said. "It is a fact that there was a change in plans."

I exploded. "YOU KNOW WHAT I MEAN!"

The flight attendant hurried over. "Girls, is everything okay?"

"No," I blurted. "We're all alone. My sister . . ."

"You are not alone," she interrupted. "I am right here." She gave her best impression of a reassuring smile. And then she sniffed the air, obviously smelling the "ode to pickle" still wafting off my skin.

"May I have another one, please?" Sunny held up her fizzy drink, smiling as if she was just an innocent six-year-old and not an evil genius wrecking her sister's life.

"Absolutely," said the flight attendant. And then she hurried away before I could ask for another fizzy drink too.

"You *ruined* the surprise!" I blurted, not letting her off the hook.

Sunny picked up her book from her lap and stuck her face into it. "Daddy e-mailed Mommy a day after the plans changed telling her that he was going on vacation in Thailand. So the surprise must not have been that important," she said, her voice smothered by the pages.

"How do you know the surprise wasn't important?" I said. As soon as those words left my mouth I wanted to scream. How did Sunny know? Sunny just knew. Sunny knew everything! I twisted with fury in my seat. But how could she know what the surprise was? She couldn't. "You can't use the scientific method to figure out a surprise," I said.

She shrugged.

Whenever Sunny chattered on and on, I wanted to strangle her. But when Sunny didn't chatter on and on—when Sunny just shrugged—I wanted to strangle her more.

The flight attendant came back with Sunny's new fizzy drink. It had two little umbrellas in it.

"So," I said, after she left. "Did you figure out the surprise?"

Sunny sipped her drink.

"Oh, now you have nothing to say?" I hissed. "Because it was a horse, right? The surprise was a horse. And now I'm never getting one." I slid hopelessly down into my seat. Not only had I lost my horse for-ever, but we were probably lost forever too. We were thousands of feet in the air heading to some place I'd never been and about to attend some camp I'd never heard of. But the most awful thing of all was that our mom and dad had no idea where we were. We were totally alone.

A laugh floated above the shhhhhing engine of the plane.

"Ho-ho-ho."

It was a big Santa-like laugh coming from a kid. And it sounded very familiar. I turned my head toward the sound. It came again.

"Ho-ho-ho."

Before my brain could figure out how I knew that laugh, Sunny turned to me. "Junchao Tao," she said.

And of course, Sunny Sweet was right.

Am I Speaking in Lizard?

I unbuckled my seat belt and leaped over Sunny, searching the sea of seats for Junchao's familiar face. Besides Santa Claus, tiny Junchao Tao was the only person I knew who had a laugh that big.

"We're descending, Masha. Bob will probably announce it in a second. I bet you're going to have to stay in your seat."

One second later Bob's voice crackled over the loudspeaker. "Ladies and gentlemen, we are heading into Portland International Jetport and should be on the ground shortly. Please take your seats and buckle in for landing."

I growled at Sunny. Then I pushed past her and took my seat. I'd find Junchao as soon as we were off this plane. I was sure her mom would help us figure this whole thing out. I sucked in a big breath of airplane air and then let it out slowly. It was all going to be okay. I didn't know how yet. But it would be.

I pictured Junchao's mother calling my father in whatever country he was in. I pictured my father rushing to the airport to get the first flight to Maine. I hoped that Toyland, or wherever he was, wasn't that long of a flight to Maine, because I was getting pretty hungry.

I spotted Junchao as soon as we left the gate. "Junchao!"

"Masha?" she said, spotting me back.

I tried to get to her, but our new unaccompanied minor attendant wouldn't let me. "You can see your friend later," she said.

"But my mother thinks we're in South Dakota and my father thinks we're, I don't know where, and I'd just call them, but my mother's in Russia and my father's in Timbuktu or something, and we . . ."

"Thailand," Sunny interrupted, smiling up at Judy, our new attendant, who had already told Sunny that she spelled her name with the traditional *y*. And then she added, "Masha only said Timbuktu because she can't remember Thailand. And Timbuktu sounds foreign and strange to her, just as Thailand does."

"You two are the funniest little kids ever," laughed Judy with a *y*.

Was I speaking Lizard? Why couldn't she understand me? This was serious.

I opened my mouth to try to explain, but Judy with a *y* sniffed the air, whispering, "I smell pickles." Then she checked the time on her phone and turned and began to walk fast. We hustled after her. I'd just have to get to Junchao and her mom at baggage claim.

The airport in Maine looked mostly like the airport in Boston . . . planes, people, rolling suitcases, and the smell of french fries and coffee in the air. We went down two escalators, following the signs for baggage that had little suitcases on them. Sunny was chattering

33

away to Judy with a *y*, telling her all these crazy statistics. I was trying not to listen to a word of it.

"American Airlines saved $40,000 in one year by removing an olive from each salad served in first class," Sunny said.

Judy with a *y* giggled away.

And, "Southwest Airlines' passengers ate 47 million bags of pretzels in one year."

Judy with a *y* turned to me and said, "Your sister is a hoot and a half."

"Yeah," I said, rolling my eyes, "if you find meaningless information a hoot." But Judy with a *y* wasn't listening to me. She was already laughing at the next "just hilarious" thing Sunny was saying.

We got to the big merry-go-rounds of baggage before our bags did. I spotted Junchao right away.

"*Ni hao*, Junchao!" I yelled.

Judy with a *y* gave me a stern look, but I ignored it. Junchao tried to head toward me, but her unaccompanied minor attendant stopped her. She said something to her attendant, and then they both started over to me. I hopped up and down with excitement . . .

until it hit me that Junchao was with an attendant, like me, and not her mother. Crud! Junchao's mother was a big part of my plan to get us out of this mess.

Junchao didn't even ask me what I was doing there. She just threw her arms around my neck in a giant hug. *"Ni rent ran wen qi lai xiang cu."* She giggled.

"Huh?"

Junchao and I had been studying Chinese together all spring. And my neighbor Mrs. Song was also helping me. But my Chinese wasn't that good yet.

"You still smell like vinegar!" Junchao said, adding her famous, "Ho-ho-ho." Then she got serious. "What are you doing here?"

"Why isn't your mom with you?" I asked.

"Why isn't your mom with you?" she asked.

"Um," I said, not knowing why Junchao would want to know where my mom was. I really must be speaking in Lizard.

The baggage belt started up. The first few suitcases dropped down the chute and onto the belt.

"Why are you alone?" I asked.

"I'm going to camp," she said. "Why are you alone?"

"We're going to camp too," said Sunny.

"No we're not," I said.

"Camp Newton?" Junchao asked. Her eyes got big and hopeful.

"Of course!" Sunny burst out. "Your mom was the one who told me about it."

"Tai bang le!" Junchao squealed and hugged me so hard I thought my teeth might pop out of my mouth. "I was really scared about going to camp for the first time all by myself," she said. "I can't believe you're here, Masha. This is the happiest day of my life."

"Junchao," I said. But she had let go of me and was running off for her bag on the belt. That's when I saw our backpacks come falling down the chute. They were bright orange and easy to spot. I had been hanging out with Alice and her physical therapist when my mom and Sunny went shopping for them. Sunny wanted us to match, so she picked out these two bright-orange backpacks with solar panels built into the back of them. She convinced my mom that it would be good if we could recharge our phones and flashlights and stuff at the dude ranch. That night at dinner I had pointed out that the brochure of the dude ranch showed a really nice hotel with beds and lamps and an Internet connection; in other words, we weren't going on an expedition to Antarctica. And also that I didn't want to match! But when I said this last part, my mom and Sunny looked at me as if I had just suggested that we starve all the kittens in the world. Anyway, I knew that Sunny chose orange for me because it was my favorite color. And I loved kittens, so I just packed my stuff in my matching, shocking, orange solar backpack. I hurried behind Junchao to pluck our backpacks from the belt.

As soon as we grabbed our bags, Judy with a *y* had us on the move. I was completely confused now. My plan had been to tell Mrs. Tao all about the mix-up, and she'd fix it. But now I didn't know what to do. All I had was *Call Alice* on my list.

"Aha!" I said. And I pulled out my cell phone and called Alice.

"Hey, Masha," she said, picking up on the second ring.

"Alice!"

"Oh no," she said. "What now?"

I only had to say her name and she knew exactly what was going on. I wasn't speaking in Lizard . . . *at least not to Alice*!

"Sunny messed up the whole trip! She told my mom that we were going to be with my dad at the dude ranch and I have no idea what she told my dad. And now I'm about to be picked up by some quacky scientist at the airport in Portland, Maine, and spend three weeks at math camp!"

"What?" Alice whispered. "You're not at the dude ranch? You're at an airport in Maine? How did she . . . Never mind. That's a silly question. Let me think."

"Okay," I said.

"Why are you all out of breath?" she asked.

"I'm following Sunny and the airport attendant out of the airport," I told her.

"To where?"

"To meet Dr. Singh. Sunny says she is in charge of the math camp."

"That's it, Masha. You need to tell this doctor everything."

"I've tried to tell people what is going on, but nobody will listen to me."

"You need to keep trying!" she said.

"Okay," I said.

"Start by saying these words: my name is Masha Sweet and there has been a big mistake."

"Okay," I said.

"You can do it, Masha," she said.

"Okay," I repeated. I wasn't that sure.

"Remember," she said. "My name is Masha Sweet and there has been a big mistake."

"Got it," I said, not feeling like I actually did.

"Now . . . I have to go. I'm about to get on Splash Mountain. And Masha, it's all going to be okay. I got you a big stuffed Eeyore."

I smiled. She knew I loved Eeyore. "Okay," I said. And this time I felt a bit more sure.

I stuck my phone back in my pocket and ran after Judy with a *y*. Sunny was dragging herself along under the heaviness of her backpack. But I didn't feel sorry for her. Her backpack was heavy because it was filled with books and science crud. I had told her to leave that stuff at home, but she wouldn't listen. The only reason she even packed underwear was because she had to wrap her glass beakers in something.

I spotted Junchao up ahead with her airport attendant. There was no reason to catch up just yet. Junchao was so happy that I'd be at the camp, and I didn't know how to tell her that I wasn't about to be going to Camp Newton! As soon as Judy with a *y* got us to the pick-up person, Dr. Singh, I would do just what Alice said and explain everything.

We finally arrived at the entrance of the gates. There was a pretty big crowd as we came through. All the people waiting looked happy and tanned in their bright summer clothes. There was lots of excited shouting and hugging. It all made me feel more alone, and I moved closer to Sunny. But then I moved away when I remembered that my dad and I could have been racing our horses across a prairie right now.

That's when I saw the sign. It was huge. It read CAMP NEWTON. And it had some squiggly symbols on it that I'm sure had something to do with math. My heart fell. Somehow I thought that this would all turn out okay—that my dad would be here, that the dude ranch was really in Maine, or that the plane had actually flown to South Dakota. Something, anything but that sign. And holding that sign was Dr. Singh.

I knew it was her. First of all, she was smiling in the same twitchy way that Sunny always did when she was thinking about math. There really, truly is a math smile. Plus she was dressed in a sari and holding the

Camp Newton sign. My third-grade teacher, Miss Verma, had been from India and had worn a sari, so I knew all about them. They were usually these bright pretty colors and floated around you like a cloud. Dr. Singh's sari was blue and heavy-looking, just like you'd think a math sari would look like.

Before I, or Judy with a *y*, could stop her, Sunny took off running for Dr. Singh. She dropped her orange solar backpack at her feet and shook Dr. Singh's hand as if she were trying to remove it from her body. Dr. Singh's smile got even bigger than when she was just standing there, holding the sign and thinking about math.

I dragged myself up to the little group of kids now surrounding Camp Newton's sign, which included Junchao. "Isn't this so great!" she whispered to me. I tried to smile. I didn't know what to say.

The other kids around us looked nervous. One of them had a solar backpack like ours, only his was in black. His looked so much cooler than ours. I waited for the other kids to say hi to Dr. Singh, and for Judy with a *y* to take off. I figured it would be better to break the bad news of the mistake to Dr. Singh without Judy with a *y* around. I was worried that she would bring up Timbuktu and Dr. Singh wouldn't listen to me.

"Okay, my Mathlings, come this way," Dr. Singh said. She had a nice voice for a scientist. She led us to the side of the crowd and, using a clipboard that she held in her hand, she took attendance. Then she smiled. It was time.

"Here goes, Alice," I whispered.

"Dr. Singh," I said. "Hi, my name is Masha Sweet and there's been a big mistake."

"Hello there, Masha," she said, so brightly that all of a sudden I hated to have to make her upset with my bad news. But there was no way around this. Sunny moved to my elbow. I could see Junchao standing off to the side of the group, watching me.

"There has been a big mistake," I repeated. "My sister and I were supposed to be in South Dakota at a dude ranch." Dr. Singh's face crunched up in confusion. This wasn't a good start.

"We're not supposed to be here," I blurted.

That was better. I could tell that she was totally listening now.

"My mom is in Russia and my father is . . . I forget where at the moment."

"Thailand," Sunny offered.

"Oh, I love Thailand," Dr. Singh said, smiling at the two of us. "It's a beautiful place."

"It's the largest producer of cars in Asia," Sunny added.

"I hadn't heard that," the doctor answered. She patted me on the head and then looked up at all of us, repeating, "Come this way, Mathlings." She turned to start walking out of the airport. "Masha, you can tell me all about Thailand and—where did you say your mother was, Russia?"

"Yes, Russia, but . . ."

"When we get to Poly." She smiled.

"Who is Poly?" someone asked.

Dr. Singh smiled again, she smiled a lot, and then she took off, leaving us Mathlings to run along behind.

It was my last chance to NOT go to math camp, and I was failing. I could see Sunny's cheeks, wide from smiling. My head felt as if it would pop right off my body. I ran to catch up to Dr. Singh. "DR. SINGH," I said, pretty loudly.

"Yes, Masha?" she asked, still hurrying toward this Poly person.

"My mother thinks we are in South Dakota with my father, and my father probably thinks we are in Russia with my mother. My little sister twisted all our plans around. My parents do not know that we are here."

She stopped walking. All the Mathlings stopped too, bumping into us.

"Your parents don't know you're here?" she asked in a worried tone, again checking her clipboard. Finally . . . an adult that understands Lizard. "But I have all the permission slips and medical histories and signatures."

"I know," I said. "That is because Sunny took care of it all."

Dr. Singh looked down at the six-year-old kid standing beside me, smiling that innocent smile of hers. "She filled out all the forms?"

"Yes," I said. I could tell that I probably should add

something else to my answer if I was going to convince her. But I was afraid that whatever I said would confuse her again.

Then Dr. Singh did the strangest thing that I'd ever seen an adult do. She turned to Sunny and asked her. "You filled out all the forms?"

"Yes," said Sunny, "but my mom signed them all."

"But . . . ," I started. Dr. Singh cut me off with a smile. And then she did the second-strangest thing I'd ever seen an adult do. She turned back to Sunny and asked a question that had to be answered in a way that made *me* look good.

"Does your mother know that you and your sister are here in Portland, Maine, and about to attend Camp Newton for three weeks?"

"W-well," Sunny stuttered. It was the most beautiful moment of my life! Dr. Singh waited. The Mathlings gathered closer. Junchao looked at me. I looked at Dr. Singh. Dr. Singh looked down at Sunny.

"No," Sunny finally said. "But . . ."

"That answer needs no qualification," Dr. Singh said, cutting Sunny off.

I didn't understand that last thing Dr. Singh said, but it didn't matter because thunder clapped and lightning flashed and the earth stopped rotating around the sun and music everywhere was silenced and merry-go-rounds creaked to a halt—well, none of this stuff really happened. But it felt like it did.

Dr. Singh had stopped Sunny Sweet in her scientific tracks, and that made her my new favorite person in the entire world!

The Gravitational Pull of Camp Newton

Dr. Singh sighed. "I'll call your mother as soon as we get to camp, Masha," she said.

Sunny's little body hunched into a heap.

Mine did too.

"Why not right now?" I asked. "Can't you put us on the next plane back to New Jersey? I'm sure my mother would want us to be heading home."

"Masha, I can't do that," Dr. Singh said. "I need to get camp started and this might take more than a few minutes to get figured out. And for the moment,

I have everything I need for you and Sunny to attend Camp Newton."

"But . . ."

"It's the only way, Masha," she said. "I will call your mother as soon as we get to camp."

I sighed and gave in.

"Let's go," Dr. Singh called.

I was on my way to Camp Newton . . . again. Sunny's smile was back. Junchao's wasn't. I headed over to walk next to her.

"*Ni hao*," I said.

"*Ni hao*," she said.

"*Dui bu qi*," I told her, which meant I was sorry. "I know you wanted me to go to camp with you."

"You would have had fun, Masha," she said.

"I know," I lied, because I would so *not* have fun at math camp. "But we are supposed to be with my father right now."

"But Sunny said he's in Thailand."

"He's only there because Sunny pretended to be my mom and made him think we couldn't go on vacation with him, so he went on vacation alone," I told her. "I know he'll come right back when he hears what's happened. And then we'll go to the dude ranch." I thought about my dad in Thailand, and I wondered for the first time why he would go there. He didn't really like to travel that much. In fact, I was sure that the only reason he was traveling to the dude ranch was so he could buy me a horse.

Just then, the double doors of the airport opened. The sky was a pretty bright pink. The sun was down, but not all the way gone yet. My stomach grumbled. It felt way past dinnertime, and I was starving. Dr. Singh led us to a very square-looking white van. "Mathlings, meet Poly," she said.

I saw Sunny take a breath to say something, but some kid standing behind us beat her to it. "I get it," he said. "Because it's the shape of a polygon."

Dr. Singh laughed. So did Sunny and all the other kids.

"That is correct, James. Now, who knows the difference between a concave polygon and a convex polygon?" asked Dr. Singh. Every single kid raised a hand. And most of them did it while making excited "pick me" sounds. Ugh, everybody here was a better Sunny than Sunny.

There were about twelve of us standing next to the van. There were more girls than boys, but it looked close to even. Most of them had glasses on. That was funny because this is what you think kids who love math would look like, and they did. Maybe I should ask my mom if I could get glasses because it might help me get better at math.

Dr. Singh opened up the back of Poly and we all tossed in our bags and suitcases. Then she popped open the doors. We climbed in and buckled up, and we were off. I sat between Sunny and Junchao.

It was quiet as we pulled out of the airport. I guess we were all feeling a little nervous. I know I was. It felt weird to be out in the world without my mom knowing where we were. Sunny must have felt it, too, because she slipped her hand into mine. I would have thrown her off me—because I was still really stinking mad at her—but I didn't. Junchao wiggled a little closer to me, and the three of us, along with all the other kids, stared out of Poly's windows as the airport slid away behind us.

After about ten minutes on the highway, I heard one of the kids sniffing. I knew what was about to come. I decided I'd meet the problem head-on. "If you smell pickles, it's me. I had to take a bath in vinegar," I announced.

I saw Dr. Singh glance over her shoulder at me from the driver's seat. The kid with the black solar backpack asked, "Did you get sprayed by a skunk?" He blinked with excitement through silver Harry Potter glasses that shined against his dark skin.

"Um," I said, "kind of." I quickly glared down at Sunny to shut her up.

"That is so cool!" he said, nodding and pushing his glasses back up on his nose. A couple of other voices seem to agree. I could feel Sunny bursting with wanting to tell everyone that she was the skunk. But I squeezed her hand and she kept quiet.

"Did you know," said a boy with heavy brown bangs sitting on the other side of Sunny, "that a skunk shoots the spray out of two glands on the side of his butt?"

Everyone groaned.

"Of course we know that," said the solar back-pack kid.

I didn't. But now I did. I smiled down at Sunny, giving her permission to admit that she was the skunk. But after what the boy with the bangs just said, I knew she wouldn't. Sunny didn't smile back.

The rest of the bus ride was taken up by a game Dr. Singh called "Name That Chemical." I stared out the window and tried to dream about riding Oscar/Charlie/Thunder/Black Cloud, but it was really hard with Sunny shouting words like "digoxin" and "batrachotoxin" in my ear.

When we arrived at the entrance to the camp, which was just a dirt road with a small wooden sign that read CAMP NEWTON, Dr. Singh made the announcement, "Here we are."

All of us turned to watch out the windows. We bounced around as Poly made her way over the dirt road, which had a lot of potholes in it. Each time we

hit one, branches of pine trees scraped at the van. Just
when it seemed that we'd never get off that road, we
pulled out into a clearing with the camp below. We all
gave a little yelp at the sight.

The valley was so pretty, with blowing long grass
that looked like the kind a lion might hide in. Pine

trees lined up around the clearing as if the trees were a picture frame and the camp was the picture. The actual camp was a bunch of wooden buildings about halfway down into the valley that were all close together like they'd gotten cold in the night and huddled into a group to keep warm. Below the buildings was a very sparkly lake stretching out like it had spilled into the pine trees. The first rays of the moon twinkled on top of the water, making it look magical. There was a beach with a long pier that stuck out into the water. I bet it would be so fun to run down it and jump off the end. My heart started beating when I saw all the tiny green little canoes lined up at one side of the lake. I'd always wanted to canoe.

Dr. Singh drove Poly down the winding dirt road, the buildings growing bigger and bigger. We pulled in front of the largest of the buildings that said MESS HALL on the front of it. It felt just like a real camp. I guess because it was.

"Everybody out," cried Dr. Singh. And slowly we unbuckled and slid open the doors and stepped out into the cool night.

The crickets were chirping. The air smelled like the ocean. Ocean air always makes me happy. But then I reminded myself that it didn't matter that this place looked fun . . . We would be out of here soon and on our way home.

We gathered our bags and backpacks and then stood around in a clump waiting for Dr. Singh's next instruction. Then someone shouted, "OUCH," and slapped his arm.

The word "mosquito" was whispered, and everyone gathered into a close clump around me, almost knocking me over. "It's just a mosquito," I said.

I heard about ten kids suck in their breath, and everybody turned to see who had said it.

"Doesn't encephalitis or dengue fever ring any bells?" asked the backpack kid.

I shook my head.

"Mosquitoes carry viruses and parasites," Sunny said.

"Whatever," I said, not really listening because I could hear dishes clanking and voices inside the building. My stomach growled. I was starving.

"You're brave," said a girl with fuzzy red hair and a strange-looking necklace. It looked like a pen on a chain.

"Thanks," I said.

"That's because she doesn't know what a parasite is and she's never seen the advanced stages of *Plasmodium falciparum*," Sunny whined. But no one was paying attention to her because Dr. Singh pointed to the entrance of the mess hall and the Mathlings were too busy stampeding toward the door. *Now who is speaking in Lizard.*

It was pretty inside the hall with bright Christmas lights strung around the roof rafters and white-painted picnic tables all in a row. The smell of wood and food floated in the air—two smells I loved. There were more campers, but not many more. And all of them stopped and stared as we came in.

"Okay," said Dr. Singh. "Put your things down here next to this table. And," she said, pointing to a line of paper bags on the table with names written in black Sharpie on them, "I'll need you each to place your phones into the bag with your name on it."

"But not us, right, Dr. Singh?" I asked.

"Yes, you two as well," she said. "At least until we work this out."

Everyone dumped their bags and pulled out their phones and put them into the bags. There was a little bit of grumbling, but not much. I guess they knew this was coming.

"Now," she said. "Go get yourselves some dinner."

This got our group moving. I guess I wasn't the only one who was starving. Everybody raced over to the open kitchen window. I hung back. Sunny and Junchao did too.

"The order of operations is food first and then phone calls to parents," Dr. Singh said.

We didn't wait for her to tell us again. The three of us ran for the back of the line. I stretched my neck to see what it was.

"Can you see?" asked Junchao. Junchao was so small that she was almost the same size as Sunny.

"Not really," I said. I was hoping for hot dogs. I'd seen a lot of movies that take place at camp, and they always have hot dogs. I love hot dogs.

We made our way up to the kitchen window, and it was hot dogs! I smiled at Sunny and she smiled back. Then I remembered that I was mad at her and miserable here and pulled my mouth into a frown.

A friendly looking lady in the kitchen handed us trays with hot dogs and funny-looking beans on them. "Beans and tofu dogs with applesauce," she said.

"What does that mean? Tofu?" I asked. "And why are the baked beans white?"

"Tofu is made from soybeans," she smiled. "And the beans are white because they're lentil beans and not navy beans. But I'd say that their color is more of a yellow than a white."

I smiled and nodded. I didn't know what the heck she was talking about. Then the three of us took our trays and headed to the tables. We sat next to the boy with the solar backpack and a girl with long dark hair.

He was already done with one of his hot dogs and was eating the second. The girl wasn't eating.

"They aren't real hot dogs," I whispered to him.

"Yeah," he said, "I know. They're tofu dogs." He took a huge bite and then spoke with his mouth full of whatever this stuff was. "The camp is vegan and gluten-free. This is my third summer at Newton."

I looked over at Sunny.

"Vegan means you don't eat animal products and gluten-free means you don't eat wheat," she said.

"Oh," I said. "I didn't know animals made products."

The girl with long dark hair laughed. "You're funny," she said.

"She's not afraid of mosquitoes either," said the kid with the backpack.

The dark-haired girl looked at me in amazement.

"That's only because she lacks information about deadly infection," said Sunny.

"I laugh at deadly infection," I said, making a muscle with one arm and pointing at it and then swatting at a pretend mosquito on it.

The dark-haired girl and the boy with the back-pack laughed again.

Sunny just rolled her eyes.

I picked up my plastic fork. I decided the only safe thing to eat was the applesauce. Sunny and I would be back at the airport in an hour, and I'd use some of the pocket money my mom gave me to buy a giant slice of pizza or something.

"How long have you been coming to this camp?" Junchao asked the girl. She was eating her fake dog. So was Sunny.

"Every single summer of my life," said the girl, shrugging. "It's my mom's camp."

"Dr. Singh is your mom?" I asked. "That's cool." I loved Dr. Singh. There aren't too many people who can best Sunny Sweet, and Dr. Singh had done it.

"So you two know each other?" Junchao asked, glancing from the kid with the solar backpack to the girl with long dark hair.

They looked at one another and smiled. "Yeah, this is Sam and I'm Riya. Sam and I are BFFs. We go to the same school back home," Riya said. Sam nodded his head as he chewed, holding his glasses on with his pointer finger.

"I'm Junchao, and this is Masha and her little sister, Sunny," Junchao said, shoving the last bite of her fake dog in her mouth. "We go to the same school back home too. And we're almost BFFs, right, Masha?" She smiled over at me.

I smiled back at Junchao, and then shoveled a big spoonful of applesauce into my mouth followed by a giant gulp of milk. I felt completely guilty because I wanted to leave here and I knew that Junchao didn't want me to. "This is good milk," I said, trying to change to the subject.

"It's made from rice," Sam said.

"Oh." I snatched my fork from the table and stuck it in my mouth, sucking the applesauce off of it to get the taste of the weird milk out of it. "Is this apple-sauce really made from apples?" I asked.

Riya laughed. "Yes, Masha, you're safe with the applesauce. And if you're still hungry later, I have a giant bag of Milky Ways hidden in my cabin."

"Thanks!" I said. But then I remembered that we

wouldn't be here later. "But," I said, frowning at Junchao, because I knew that this was going to make her sad, "Sunny and I aren't staying. We're not supposed to be here."

I did my best to explain what Sunny had done while my little sister smiled proudly next to me. Sam and Riya listened with wide, staring eyes. Junchao ate my white beans. She wasn't that interested in the story because she was already used to the crazy stuff that Sunny Sweet did.

When I got to the part where I told Dr. Singh in the airport, the doctor showed up in the mess hall and came and sat at our table. "Would you three mind finishing up at another table?" she asked, looking at Riya, Sam, and Junchao. "I need to speak with Masha and Sunny."

The three of them stood up with their trays and moved to the table next to us. Before Dr. Singh said anything, I heard Riya say she smelled pickles. And then I heard Junchao give one of her famous "ho-ho-hos," and I knew that Junchao would be all right here at the camp without me. This sent a very strange thought through my head, that I was jealous of Junchao that she got to stay and eat Milky Ways with Riya and Sam later.

Focus, I told myself. *Think about Oscar/Charlie/ Thunder/Black Cloud.*

"Well?" I asked. "When will my dad be here?"

"Three weeks," Dr. Singh said.

"WHAT?" I shouted.

"Masha," Dr. Singh started. "Everything is going to be fine."

I put my head in my hands so I didn't have to see Sunny Sweet gloating at her victory over me, but also because about a fountain of tears threatened to burst from my eyes. "Why isn't our dad coming?" I choked.

"Masha," Dr. Singh said quietly. She did have the nicest voice. But it just made stopping my tears even harder. "I couldn't get ahold of your mother just yet, as she hasn't landed in Russia. But thanks to your neighbor, Mrs. Song, I was able to get in touch with your grandmother in Russia. As you know, your mother is there for her hip surgery, which is happening in the next day or two. I was then able to get ahold of your father through the hotel information that he gave on our forms."

"Then why isn't he com . . ." I couldn't get the rest of the word out of my mouth without falling to a billion pieces right into my plate of counterfeit food.

"Sunny," Dr. Singh said, "why don't you go sit with Sam and Riya for a few minutes."

"Please," Sunny begged, "I want to stay with Masha."

Dr. Singh looked at me. "It turns out, Masha, that your father did know about you and Sunny attending Camp Newton. In fact, he was shocked that you and your mother didn't know about it. He said that he and your mother had been e-mailing. And that your mother wasn't thrilled with the surprise he was going to give to you and your sister. She asked him to change the summer plans. He said that they decided together, through e-mail, to send you to Camp Newton."

Both of us turned to look at Sunny.

Sunny gave a little shrug.

I couldn't help it then. A gasping cry fell from my mouth. "You did this!" I hissed at her. "Why? Why did you do this? Because you didn't want me to have a horse?"

"The surprise . . . ," she said.

"What? What about the surprise?" I practically screamed.

Sunny's bottom lip shook, and I just about lost it. She wasn't allowed to mess up my life and then make me feel sorry for her!

Dr. Singh put her hand on my arm. "The solution to the problem is this, Masha," she explained, smiling that nice smile of hers that I liked even though I was totally mad right now. "Your mother will know that you are with us when she gets to Russia. Your father already knows that you're here with us, and he will come pick you up at the end of camp. And girls," she said firmly, "my theory is that you are going to have a good time here with us. And that theory has been rigorously proven within a formal system."

Sunny giggled at the dumb science joke, but I didn't get it. What I did get was this: *I was about to experience the worst three weeks of my life, and as usual, it was all Sunny's fault!*

Binary Relationship

"Why can't she bunk with the other little kids?" I asked.

Riya, Junchao, Sunny, and I stumbled along a trail that led off a dirt road about a five-minute walk from the mess hall. The trail was filled with tiny stones that sounded nice as we crunched over them in the dark.

"She's the only little kid," said Riya. "These three weeks are for kids from ten to thirteen years old. And then my mother runs a four-week camp for high school kids. Sam got to come before he was ten so he could keep me company because I had to come. Otherwise, no one Sunny's age is allowed. She is here because she petitioned my mother for admission through her experiments in radiant energy. My mother went on the hypothesis that you and Sunny would want to bunk together because you're sisters."

I turned to look at Sunny walking behind me, her orange backpack glowing brightly in the dark, as I'm sure mine was. She stared back at me with those giant eyes of hers, and I swallowed the first group of words that were about to come out of my mouth: *Your mother thought wrong.* I also swallowed the second group of words: *Why is Sunny allowed here if she isn't old enough?* I knew the answer to this better than I knew what my own nose looked like. Sunny Sweet was always allowed everywhere.

"Masha and I are a binary relationship," Sunny said.

Riya and Junchao laughed. I didn't.

"A binary relation is a mathematical relationship involving two elements," Sunny told me.

"I know what it is," I snapped, even though I didn't.

Riya led the way with a flashlight while the three

of us lugged our backpacks behind her. We could hear happy shouts and laughter coming from all around us in the dark. Everyone was glad to be here at Camp Math. Well . . . almost everyone.

The trail led toward a line of tiny wooden cabins. On the front of each cabin next to the door was a light. The lights made them look like tiny homes. Ours was the second from the right. We clonked up the four wooden steps.

"Do we just live here alone?" I asked.

"We sleep in here alone," Riya said. "But we're not alone. A camp counselor is assigned to us and stays in the next cabin over. Her name is Molly, and she does like a million bed checks every night." When Riya opened the screen door, it creaked as loud as the floorboards do in front of Mrs. Song's stove. We followed her inside.

It smelled green and woody, and I sucked in a big smell of it. But then I remembered I hated it here and tried to unsmell it.

There were two bunk beds on either side of the

room. One square window faced out the back of the
cabin. And there were hooks and shelves at the foot of
each set of beds. One of the beds was made up with a
green sleeping bag and a red-and-black-checked
blanket folded at the end of it.

I looked at Riya. "We don't have sleeping bags."

"Don't worry," she said, walking to the shelves by

the bunk beds that weren't made up. She pulled sheets and blankets down and tossed them on the bottom bunk.

"This place is great," Junchao said. "I'll take the top bunk with Riya!" Then she dropped her backpack and ran to look out the little back window. "Oh no, there's a latrine."

"What's a latrine?" I asked. "And where's the bathroom?"

"The word 'latrine' comes from the Latin word *lavare*, which means to wash," Sunny said.

"That didn't answer my question," I said.

"Did you know," started Junchao, "that the word 'toilet' comes from the French *toilette*, which means dressing room?"

"Yes," Riya said, falling onto her bunk bed. "But do you know where the word *toilette* comes from?"

"It comes from the French word *toile*, which means cloth," Sunny said.

I was bunking with Wikipedia.

"And by the way," said Riya to me, "latrine just means bathroom."

"But why is the bathroom out back and not in the cabin?" I asked.

"Because this is camp," Riya said.

"And at camp," Junchao said, frowning, "you have to go to the bathroom with your flashlight and brush your teeth pretty much out in the woods. I was hoping that we'd have real facilities at Camp Newton."

"I think that sounds kind of fun," I said before I could stop myself. Sunny glanced at me and I gave her the stink eye, which is just a funny name for a mean stare. She was the big fat reason I was horseless right at the moment, and I was never going to let her forget it.

"Let's make our beds and unpack," Junchao suggested.

We made our beds and put away our clothes on the shelves. I was careful not to show it, but it was kind of cool folding my shorts and T-shirts and socks in little piles on the shelves. When I was rearranging my T-shirts by color, I found a stack of brochures for the camp stacked in the back of my top shelf. I sat down on my bunk and began to flip through one. There was a picture of a kid at bat.

"When do we play softball?" I asked.

Riya was helping Junchao make up her bunk. She gave a snort.

There were a bunch of pictures of kids swimming in the lake. "Are we allowed to run down the pier and jump off?" I asked.

"You mean, into the water?" asked Riya.

"I can't swim," Junchao said.

"Yes," I said, "into the water."

Again Riya snorted.

"I guess not." I sighed. "That's okay. I like just running into the water straight from the beach too," I told her.

"Masha," Riya said. "We're here to test the water in the lake, not swim in it."

"I read through Camp Newton's labs from last year," Sunny said. "The rate of algae growth in the lake has doubled in the last decade. I don't know if you'd want to swim with that much algae."

Junchao gave a soft "Ho-ho-ho" and then let out a sigh.

"What about the canoes?" I asked, feeling like I might already know the answer to my question.

Riya looked across the cabin at me and smiled. "No one ever goes canoeing at Camp Newton."

"Then why are they all lined up down there?"

"Every year, our groundskeeper, Mr. Ross, gets the camp ready for us. And every year he puts them out. They just came with the camp when my mom bought it."

I frowned and put down the brochure.

"Let's get this latrine visit over with," Junchao suggested. I could tell she was trying to change the subject. She walked to the door in her pajamas and sneakers, holding her toothbrush and toothpaste in one hand and a can of insect repellent in the other.

Riya grabbed a bucket from off her shelf. Her toothbrush and toothpaste clanked together inside it.

I quickly fished mine out of my backpack. I liked the idea of having to walk outside in the night to brush my teeth. It was an adventure.

"I'm just going to set up my glass beakers and

graduated cylinders. I'll brush mine tomorrow," Sunny said. She started pulling little bottles out of her backpack.

"Get your toothbrush and come on," I told her. Sunny hated to brush her teeth. I don't know why. But it was gross.

"And Sunny," Riya said, "my mom doesn't like chemicals in the cabins."

Sunny grabbed her toothbrush. "I e-mailed her a list of what I was bringing. She approved everything. I need to continue my work outside the lab if I'm going to get everything done."

"Everything done?" Riya asked.

"Don't bother asking," I said. "Let's just go."

Riya opened the cabin door and there was that loud creak again. I liked the sound. It was a happy sound, and before I could stop myself, I smiled. Sunny caught me and smiled back. I turned away from her and followed Riya and Junchao down the cabin steps and out onto the path. It wound in a circle around the row of cabins. As we passed the cabin next to ours, a head full of dark braids popped out the door. "Destination?"

"Latrine," Riya answered. And then to us, she whispered, "Molly."

"Singh, Tao, Sweet, Sweet?" Molly demanded.

"Confirmed," answered Riya.

"Proceed," said Molly's head as she pulled herself back into the cabin.

"Molly wants to be a Marine one day," Riya told us as we made our way past the last cabin.

All around us shouts and laughter came from the cabins, and white balls of light bobbed between the trees as other kids made their way places. Everyone had flashlights. Riya said we could buy them at the camp store in the morning when it opened. I liked the idea of going to the store by myself and buying stuff. My mom had given Sunny and me each some summer money to spend on anything we wanted. I had bought a cheeseburger and french fries at the airport with some of mine already. If only I had that cheeseburger right now! Sunny didn't spend a single penny of hers. I'm sure she's saving it all up for some sort of freeze gun or gamma ray because that is what evil scientists do.

A big moth flew past. Junchao screeched and ducked, spraying repellant.

"It's just a moth," I said, ducking out of the way of the yucky-smelling spray.

"Actias luna," said Sunny from behind us.

"I hate insects," Riya said.

"Me too," Junchao moaned.

"I thought it was kind of pretty," I told them. "How do you say moth in Chinese, Junchao?"

"*Zhu*," she grumbled.

"*Zhu, zhu, zhu*," I repeated a few times under my breath so I would remember it.

We marched around the cabins, crunching stones as we walked. Riya led with Junchao following two inches from Riya's back, her head swiveling around on her neck watching out for more *zhus*. Sunny came next. And then me.

The crickets chirped. Fireflies blinked on and off all around us. The nighttime air smelled sweet and tasted like a million secrets. The trees and bushes glowed white in the moonlight. I felt like I might be glowing too, although I didn't know what color.

We turned a little corner and there were the latrines. Over one doorway it read GIRLS and over the other, BOYS. Junchao stopped at the entrance, her face crinkled in a frown.

"Here," I said, "give me your spray and I'll go in and get the bugs out."

Junchao's face uncrinkled. She handed me her spray. "Thanks, Masha."

"Yeah, thanks, Masha," Riya repeated.

I walked into the latrine. It was wooden inside like all the other buildings. It had a long sink along one wall and lots of stalls. Some looked like shower stalls, but most of them were toilet stalls. It smelled like horrible cleaning stuff that burned my nose. There were windows all along the top, but they had no glass in them. It was totally open to the woods outside. And because of this, there were a lot of bugs. Just spraying them dead seemed so mean, so instead, I sprayed the air below them, shooing them all out of the open windows.

"All clear," I announced, stepping out of the latrine. There was a little crowd of girls now standing with Junchao, Riya, and Sunny.

"Masha got all the bugs out for us," Junchao announced.

There was a murmuring of "wows" and "cools" and "greats" as the girls filed past me into the latrine, smiling. I heard someone ask if I was Masha Sweet, the girl who wasn't afraid of mosquitoes. And then I heard someone else say that I was. It made me feel a little embarrassed to be talked about, but I liked it.

Sunny stood outside with me. "Go in," I told her.

She didn't move. Instead, she frowned. "But we're a binary relationship," she said.

"Well this half of the math joke wishes she were at the Lone Creek Dude Ranch right now," I snapped. "Go." And she went.

I took a big breath of night air and thought about what Sunny had done. I wasn't at the Lone Creek

Dude Ranch right now. I was at math camp. I looked down the hill through the dark trees while I listened to the girls laughing and talking in the latrine. Did I really wish I were at the Lone Creek Dude Ranch? I could just make out the green canoes shining like a row of unripe bananas in the moonlight. I thought about Oscar/Charlie/Thunder/Black Cloud and how I wasn't going to get to ride him this summer and a big sigh fell out of me. I looked back down at those canoes. They weren't as good as a horse . . . but they might be fun. Then I heard someone call my name, "Masha, aren't you coming in?" followed by more voices, "Yeah, come on."

I laughed. "Coming," I called.

Multiplications

I woke up with my nose squished up against the cabin wall.

"Sunny," I moaned, "move over."

My little sister didn't budge. I rolled over the top of her and out of the bunk. It's not the first time Sunny has crept into bed with me at night. When my dad and mom first divorced and we moved from Pennsylvania to New Jersey, Sunny crawled into bed with me every night for two months. I could say that I hated it, but I didn't. I liked waking up with her fuzzy, red footie pajamas snuggled up next to me. But that was before she decided to ruin the biggest surprise of my life!

Junchao and Riya were both sleeping lumps in their bunks.

"I'm going to the latrine, Sunny," I whispered.

Sunny yawned and sat up.

"You coming?" I asked.

"No," she said. "I have to get to work on my project."

"Really?" I asked. "Right now?" But Sunny didn't answer. She was already out of bed and pulling science junk from her clothes shelf.

A snort came from across the room and then the swish of blankets. Junchao was up and out of her bunk. "*Wo ye shi*," she said. I knew that meant "me too" in Chinese, but even if I hadn't known it, I would have understood that Junchao did not want to go to the latrine alone.

"Riya?" I asked.

"Go on," Riya said, with her eyes still closed. "I don't like insects, but I'm not as scared as Junchao." She giggled.

"I'm not scared," Junchao said.

Riya opened her eyes and looked at Junchao.

"I guess I am," said Junchao, and then she laughed. "Ho-ho-ho!" Which made all of us laugh . . . until Sunny smiled up at me from the tools of her evil trade and I stopped.

Junchao and I made our way to the bathroom and back, getting stopped both ways by Molly to give her a report.

"Be in the mess hall by 0800 hours," she barked.

"Yes, sir!" I said, even though I had never heard of that time before. Junchao saluted. And then we clomped up the steps to our cabin to get dressed.

"Pancakes!" I yelled when I saw what was for breakfast. The four of us had run the entire way to the mess hall. It was fun to run on the little paths. I got there second, after Riya.

"*Idlis*," said Sam. He was already eating.

"Is that another name for pancakes?" I asked, even though I was getting used to asking hopeful questions about camp that I already knew the hopeless answers to.

"*Idlis* are cakes made from rice and beans," Sunny

said. "There was a picture of them in the brochure I showed you on the plane, Masha."

My heart fell . . . burrito pancakes?

"Try them," Riya urged, taking a plateful. "They taste really good."

"What's this brown stuff on the side?" I asked.

"It smells like chutney," said Junchao.

"It is," Riya said, smiling.

I sniffed the chutney. "It smells a little good," I said. "What is it?"

Sunny took a breath, but I cut her off. "Don't say a word," I told her. "I decided that I don't want to know what this is. I'm just going to eat it."

We all laughed.

Dr. Singh walked into the mess hall at that very moment. I quickly smothered my laughter, pulled my eyebrows together, and turned my mouth into a giant fishlike frown. I didn't want to prove Dr. Singh's theory, *that I would have a good time here at Camp Newton*, on my very first morning! But I knew she saw me laughing. I could tell by the way she walked past us without looking at us but with her eyes all wide.

Dr. Singh made her way up to the front of the mess hall and called all the camp counselors to her. She then passed out a bunch of papers to each. The

counselors headed out into the rows of picnic tables with the papers, reading the names at the top of the paper and then handing them to the campers. Molly handed one to Riya, and then to Junchao, and then to Sunny, and then to me.

"Okay, Mathlings, you will see on your schedules that we were able to give you most of your top choices in courses," Dr. Singh announced.

"Our choices?" I whispered.

"Don't worry," Sunny said, looking up from her schedule. "I picked good choices for you."

Oh great, I'm sure I'll have a ton of fun for three weeks in Sunny's "good" choices.

The World of Enzymes
Biotechnology Level 1
Fundamentals of Location Technology Level 1
Urban Landscapes

"What the heck is an enzyme?"

I quickly looked up as Junchao, Riya, and Sunny all opened their mouths. I held up my hand. "From now on, whenever I ask a question I don't want an answer," I told them.

Looking back at my schedule, I wondered about Urban Landscapes. I admitted to myself that this one might be good. I knew that urban meant city and landscapes probably had to do with the buildings. Building cities sounded kind of fun. But when I looked at the rest of it, all I saw was embarrassing Level Ones and no time for swimming or canoeing. Maybe Riya really wasn't kidding about that stuff.

I glanced over at Sunny's schedule. The first course was Surgical Techniques in the Wilderness. I immediately got a vision of Sunny Sweet standing in the woods and holding a scalpel. "Let me see that," I said, swiping at her schedule. Sunny whisked it out of my reach.

"So," Dr. Singh called out, "you now have your schedules. Any questions?"

No one raised a hand or said anything.

My hand hovered by my shoulder. It then moved up even with my ear. When my fingers reached up over the top of my head . . . Dr. Singh saw it.

"Masha?"

"Um, Dr. Singh, um. When do we swim?"

There was a little laughter, but mostly just sniffling

and shuffling and a whole lot of wide-open eyes look-ing from me to Dr. Singh and then back to me. Dr. Singh turned her head to the side, thinking. It seemed as if I'd stumped her.

Sunny spoke up, "There's a high concentration of algae in the lake."

"Can that hurt you?" I asked.

"Not really," Dr. Singh answered. I waited a second, but when she didn't say anything else, I asked again.

"So, when do we go swimming?"

"No one probably even has a bathing suit," Junchao mumbled.

"We do," I told her.

"I do," said Riya, smiling at her mom.

"I do too," said Sam. "My mom makes me pack my bathing suit every year even though I tell her that I don't use it."

The room broke out in chatter. It seemed there were a lot of moms that made kids pack their bath-ing suits, and a bunch of other stuff, too, that was unnecessary here.

"Okay, okay," Dr. Singh said, holding up her hand to get our attention. "Perhaps right before lunch we can fit in a half hour down at the beach."

There were a couple of moans, but mostly there were a bunch of quiet yeses.

"But that time cuts directly into my Independent Study of Survival Training," Sunny complained.

"Survival what?" I asked, trying to snatch her schedule again. Sunny stuffed it in her shorts pocket.

"Now, now, everyone, calm down. It's just a half hour," Dr. Singh said. "And who knows, maybe it will be fun?" She looked very hard at me when she said this. Of course I got her big fat hint that I needed to *try* Camp Newton before I decided it wasn't for me. I saw my chance and jumped in about the canoes.

"Can we ride in the canoes too?" I asked.

Riya gasped.

"One thing at a time, Masha," Dr. Singh said. "Now, let's get moving to our first classes."

As I shuffled off to the World of Enzymes, campers gave me high fives and thumbs-up. Some said, "Way to go, Masha." And others just smiled. I smiled back, not caring if Dr. Singh or Sunny Sweet saw me having a good time. I even smiled halfway through the World of Enzymes, but then the happiness wore off because I was in the World of Enzymes, and after an hour of class I still didn't really know what an enzyme was. It was something small. I got that much.

Biotechnology was better. We talked about cells, which also turned out to be small. So far, it looked like I'd be spending three weeks studying tiny things. But the best part of the bio course was that it was time to swim when it was over. I was the first one to rip off my lab coat and run to the cabin to get my suit. Riya and Sunny and Junchao showed up five minutes later.

"Let's go, let's go," I said.

"I'm just gonna watch," Junchao sighed.

"I can teach you to swim, Junchao," Riya said.

"I don't have a bathing suit," Junchao told her, looking a little too happy about it.

"I have an extra one." I whipped out my blue bathing suit and tossed it to Junchao. This time, Junchao's sigh was louder and longer.

"Come on," I told her. "Try. I'm trying this camp."

"That's because you have to," Junchao snapped.

"Well, that is kind of true," I admitted. "But I'm still trying."

Junchao stared at me for a second. "I don't think I can do it, Masha."

"I'm not going swimming either," said Sunny.

"Yes you are," I said, throwing her bathing suit at her.

"You can bring a horse to water, but you can't make him drink," she said.

"DON'T YOU DARE TALK ABOUT HORSES!" I shouted. "Now put on that suit and let's go. You'll be lucky if I don't feed you to the sharks."

"It's freshwater," Sunny said, putting on her suit.

"Whatever," I said.

"Cabin sixteen, atten-CHUN!" yelled Molly from outside our screen door. "I need the Sweets front and center."

I threw Junchao a "please, please," look and then Sunny and I picked up our towels and scrambled out of the cabin.

"Dr. Singh wants you two in her office, stat!" cried Molly.

My heart fell. I hoped this wasn't about swimming.

Sunny and I walked to Dr. Singh's office. When we got there, the door was open and Dr. Singh was on the phone. She looked up and motioned us inside. "Yes, yes, they're here," she said into the phone. "Your mom," she mouthed to us and then clicked the phone on speaker.

"Masha? Sunny?" the phone cackled.

"Mom!" I shouted, while missing her hit me in the gut like a hard-kicked rubber kickball.

"Oh, my *malyshka*, I'm so sorry about the mix-up. How are you?" my mother breathed into the phone.

Mix-up. How could she label Sunny's latest scheme using words that made it sound like someone put sugar in your tea instead of honey? I wanted to answer her, but somehow no words would come out of my mouth.

Dr. Singh jumped in. "They're about to go swimming in the lake," she offered.

"I don't want to swim," Sunny said.

I heard my mother laugh.

"It was Masha's idea," added Dr. Singh.

"Masha?" my mother said. "How are you, honey?"

It was an easy question, but I could hear that it was filled with lots of hard stuff inside it. My eyes got wet and my chest tightened and I wanted to shout something like *How could you let Sunny ruin our surprise and take me all the way to Maine . . . ? And where are you . . . ? And I was scared on the plane without you . . . And why did you and Daddy have to divorce anyway, because none of this would have happened if we were back at our real home in Pennsylvania, and I wouldn't be standing here in this strange place?* But then I looked up, and just as a couple of tears slid over the lids of my eyes, I saw Junchao and Riya standing at the office door, *and Junchao was wearing my blue bathing suit!* She shrugged her tiny shoulders and smiled. Riya waved at me to hurry up.

"I'm great," I mumbled. And I heard my mother let out a big breath. "Um," I said. "How is Babushka's hip?"

"They will fix her hip tomorrow morning. She sends you both hugs and kisses. And Masha," she said,

"Babushka is really happy I'm here." I could tell she was smiling when she said it. "Now go and have fun in the lake, and I'll see you very soon. I love you."

"LOVE YOU BACK," shouted Sunny.

"Me too." I laughed.

I heard her breathe one last time before she hung up. The hollow sound of the phone clicking off made me feel as if I'd just been tagged in freeze tag, and I stood staring down at Dr. Singh's pencils on her desk. Dr. Singh gave my arm a squeeze. "Good job, Masha," she whispered.

"Let's go. Let's go," Riya huffed.

"I don't want to go," Sunny said.

"Everybody's going, including you, Sunny," said Dr. Singh.

Riya came and grabbed my hand and pulled me out of the office, and then the three of us ran down to the lake. Dr. Singh and Sunny walked.

Standing on the beach, Dr. Singh gave us the rules before we could go in. The lake water looked so dark blue and pretty that I stopped thinking about my mom and started thinking about playing Marco Polo.

But there were a lot of rules to go through.

Mostly they came down to no one getting to go in the water past their knees since none of us had been tested for swimming. Anyone who wanted to go deeper needed to test. And that wouldn't happen today.

By the time Dr. Singh was done with her speech, all the campers were sitting down on their towels or digging in the rocky sand at the shore. Sunny was busy playing behind me with two rocks and not listening to the water speech at all.

Finally, Dr. Singh gave us the go ahead. "All Mathlings now have permission to enter the water."

Not a single camper made a move.

Riya and I blinked at one another. Dr. Singh looked around at all of us, her eyebrows raised. Someone had to take the plunge. If I did, maybe no one would follow me in and I'd be the only one in the water. And then maybe this would be the last time Dr. Singh would let us swim. The beach was silent except for Sunny slapping her two silly rocks together over and over. "Cut it out," I told her.

"I'm creating friction," she said, continuing to bash her rocks together.

"I don't . . . ," I said, but before I could finish, a tiny light leaped from Sunny's rocks and hit me right in the butt, and it *burned*! I leaped up with a howl.

Everyone stared at me for two heartbeats. And then they *all* leaped up with a howl.

Laughing, I made for the water. And when I came

up for air, I was being stampeded by campers splashing in. I shouted and fell back in with as big a splash as I could. The water was cold and soft and great. Sam came up behind me and tagged my toe.

"You're it!"

I jumped after him through the water. The girl with the pen for a necklace joined in. And then so did a bunch of other kids.

After a while of playing, I swam up to Junchao and Riya at the edge of the lake like a crocodile.

"Don't splash us," Junchao said. "I'm busy *trying*."

"*Gui mi*," I said.

Junchao smiled down at me.

Riya looked back and forth between me and Junchao.

"It means 'best girl friend' in Chinese," Junchao told her. "*Gui mi*, Riya,"

"*Gui mi*, Junchao," Riya said.

I spit a big mouthful of water filled with algae at the two of them. They laughed and splashed me away.

I found Sunny sitting in the sand. It looked like

Dr. Singh had taken her rocks away. "Sorry about burning your butt," she said.

"No you're not."

Sunny giggled.

A half hour ago in Dr. Singh's office I could have strangled Sunny Sweet. But not now. Drying in the sun at the water's edge and listening to the campers laughing and splashing around behind me and knowing that it was because I raised my hand, well, I just wasn't in the mood.

"Want to identify minerals from sand particles with me?" Sunny asked. "You can use mineral identification to help navigate if you're lost in the wilderness."

"I don't plan on being lost in the wilderness." I laughed.

"Masha!" someone called from the water.

And then someone else shouted, "Masha, come in!"

I jumped up, ran across the little beach, and threw myself into the lake.

Eureka!

On my third morning in the World of Enzymes, I was struggling to keep my eyes open. Sunny had been sneaking into my bunk late at night after staying up to study and then tossing and turning her way to sleep. Whatever all these special projects were that she was working on, they sure were keeping us both up all night. Just when I was about to drift off, Riya walked in.

"Sorry to interrupt, Dr. Kassab," she said. "My mom asked me to get these files out of here." Riya walked to the back of the room toward two boxes.

"Can I help her?" I asked, jumping up from the table.

"*May* I help her," said Dr. Kassab.

"Oh, yeah, sure. Of course you can, Dr. Kassab," I said, sitting back down.

"No, no, Masha, I was just pointing out the correct usage," she said, "as in the difference between ability and permission."

"Does that have something to do with enzymes?" I asked.

Dr. Kassab just smiled. "Why don't you help Riya with those boxes, Masha?"

I jumped back up and grabbed a box. I was so outta there.

"Not feeling the enzymes today, huh?" Riya said as we headed for her mom's office.

I rolled my eyes.

"Help me file these. Then you won't have to go back at all," she suggested.

"Sure!"

Dr. Singh's office always smelled like coffee. It was also mostly neat, but with lots of papers on her desk and about a million pencils stuffed in coffee cans, and they were all sharpened really pointy. Riya laughed when she noticed me noticing them. "Sharpening pencils helps my mom think."

"Maybe I should try it?" I said. "I'm always looking for ways to get better at math and science other than actually learning anything about them."

Again Riya laughed. "You're funny, Masha." I never got tired of Riya saying that.

Riya started unpacking the files. I jumped in to help. I'd do just about anything to keep from going back to enzyme class.

"Do you like math and science?" I asked. "Some of your mom must have worn off onto you." I passed Riya folders full of papers and she sorted them into the cabinets.

"Has Sunny worn off on you?" she said.

"Ha!" I said, laughing. "You got me."

"Anyway," Riya whispered, holding onto the folder I passed her for a second. "I do like math and science. I actually think I want to be an engineer when I grow up. But because my mom would be so happy if she knew, I try not to let her know."

"Does that make sense and I just don't get it?" I asked. "Because that happens a lot to me."

Riya laughed. "No, Masha, I guess it doesn't make total sense. It's just that . . . if she knew that I wanted to be an engineer, she would be *so happy*. And then I wouldn't be able to change my mind, you know, if I decided to study something else. Because if I did decide that I wanted to study something else, she'd be so sad."

"I get it," I told her. "You are disappointing her now just in case you have to disappoint her later."

Riya giggled. "Yes, that's it!"

"Well," I said, "at least you have the skills to maybe make your mom happy one day."

"You have skills too," Riya said.

"Not if you ask the enzymes, I don't."

"You're not afraid of insects. And you talked my mom into letting us swim every day," she said, still holding that same folder.

"Your mom just let us do that because she wanted me to be happy. That way, later she can say that I did have a good time at Camp Newton."

"And are you?" she asked.

"Put that folder away," I said, "before the paper turns yellow with age." I wasn't ready to admit that besides enzyme class and the tofu shaped as food, Camp Newton was pretty fun. I loved the smell of the woods, the kids were completely awesometastic, and whispering with Riya and Junchao all night about school, and which color sneakers are the best, and what we'd each eat if someone paid us, was so much fun.

Riya read the file name: "Softball Statistics, file under *S*."

"Wait," I said, grabbing it from her. "Softball?" I opened the file, but all it had was pages and pages of numbers. "How is this about softball?"

"Each year we play Falcon Hill Camp, the camp across the lake, in a game of softball the last week of camp."

"Wow, I thought you said we didn't play. I'm going to try out for my softball team at school this year, so this is great," I said. "When do we start practicing?"

"We don't start practicing," Riya said, grabbing the

next file, reading its label, and then putting it into the cabinet.

"Don't you like softball?"

"I love softball. And I love basketball and volleyball and field hockey and ice hockey, and I even love running track."

"Do you play all those sports?"

"I don't play any of them . . . at least not outside of gym class."

"Why not?"

"I don't know. I guess because I have three older brothers and none of them played. And my dad, he's doing research in Germany this summer, he doesn't play any sports either."

"And so that means you can't?"

"I just think my parents would see it as a waste of homework and study time." Riya sighed.

"But it's summer," I said, sitting down at Dr. Singh's desk with the softball file, "which is the official period to waste time, right?"

"This is Camp Newton, Masha. We don't play softball for the same reason we don't swim," she said. "Or didn't swim," she corrected. "We're here to calculate ball trajectory, not learn how to actually hit balls."

"Can't we be here for both?"

She shrugged. "We've been playing this game against Falcon Hill since before I can remember. And one thing I do remember is that we've never won."

"Why do you write this stuff down, then?"

"It's my mother's way to make the time count."

"Can't it just count as fun?"

"It's not fun," Riya said. "Trust me."

We laughed.

I filtered back through the notebook. "These numbers go all the way back to the 1990s!"

"What numbers?" asked Sam.

Riya and I looked up. "Hi, Sam," Riya said.

Sam came around the side of the desk. I spread the file out before him. "Oh," he said, looking kind of glum. "Dr. Singh makes us play."

"Would you rather be sitting on the bench writing all these numbers?" I asked.

"YES!" Sam said. "All the campers would rather be taking stats."

"But if everyone at Camp Newton wants to be writing numbers during the softball game, who plays?" I asked.

Sam groaned. "Dr. Singh holds a lottery. The 'winners' of the lottery have to play." He said "winners" with a whine. "It's definitely not winning. Remember the last time I had to play?" he said, looking at Riya.

"A grade-two concussion from a wild pitch," Riya informed me.

107

"Why weren't you wearing a helmet?" I gasped. The whole reason I wanted to join the Seward Elementary softball team were the blue helmets. Everyone looked so cool in them walking up to home plate. I couldn't wait to wear one.

"He was wearing a helmet," Riya said.

"Falcon Hill is that good?" I asked.

"All I know is, we are that bad," Sam said.

"What are we bad at?" Dr. Singh walked into her office with Sunny close behind her.

"Softball," said Sam.

"Well, bad is a relative term," Dr. Singh noted.

"Camp Newton is bad at softball by anyone's definition, Mom," Riya said. "We have never scored a single run in all the years we've played."

Sunny skipped over and started flipping through the sheets of statistics.

"But," said Dr. Singh, holding up a finger, "we learned a lot about calculation, measurement, logic, probability . . ."

"What does any of that have to do with softball?" I asked.

Dr. Singh frowned.

"It looks like you need to adjust how you approach your on-base percentage," said Sunny.

We all looked at her.

"It would improve the . . ."

"Sunny's right," Sam said, scanning the statistics.

Ugh . . . if I only had a dollar for every time I heard that. "We're talking about playing softball, Sunny. Not about doing math."

"In math, you seek out patterns and then formulate ideas based on them. Mathematical reasoning can provide insight into what will happen next, like where a ball is likely to be hit and who is likely to hit it the farthest," she said.

"So in other words, math can help us win the softball game this year against Falcon Hill Camp?" I asked.

Sunny eyed the statistics again. "No," she said. "The odds are totally against Camp Newton."

"Sunny," I groaned.

"If you did everything the numbers told you to do, you might be able to get a single run," Sunny said.

"That's great!" I said. "A run is all we need. A run is just like winning."

"One run is not winning, Masha," Riya said. "There is winning and there is losing. Both are clearly defined. And at Camp Newton, we are not winners."

"I'm not sure I would support that statement," said Dr. Singh.

"So you think that if we get one run, we've won, Dr. Singh?" I asked.

"Yes," she said, smiling. "I think if we set a goal for one run and then accomplished this goal, then we have won."

"It looks like Riya's statistics for getting a hit are highest," Sunny said, staring down at the numbers on the page.

"It's called a batting average," Sam said.

Riya smiled but then tried to smother it in a shrug as she looked over at her mother.

"EUREKA!" I shouted. "How about Sam and Riya and I figure out how to get our run? And then we can hold practices with the whole camp!" I said.

"The word 'eureka' should be saved for big discoveries," said Sunny. "Overuse dilutes its meaning."

"This *is* a big discovery."

"It's definitely a cool discovery," said Riya.

"And I love statistics!" Sam smiled.

"EUREKA!" the three of us shouted.

Sunny shrugged at the three of us and then walked over to Dr. Singh's office window and opened it. She reached out the window and pulled a thermometer out of a drainpipe that was just outside the windowsill. After checking it, she shut the window and scribbled something in a little notebook that she took from her pocket.

"Sunny, aren't you supposed to be in Advanced Complex Trait Genetics right now?" asked Dr. Singh.

"I'm just checking in with my North American Climate experiment. It's part of my independent study," Sunny answered.

"How many independent studies did I approve for you?" Dr. Singh frowned.

"Six," Sunny said.

Dr. Singh laughed and then took Sunny by the

shoulders and began to lead her out of the office. Before Dr. Singh left, she turned to us. "Well," she said, "I think that one run is a great idea. But you will need your friend Junchao's help, Sam. She is an excellent statistician. I loved her report on the statistics of sound frequencies she sent with her camp application."

"Thanks, Dr. Singh. This is going to be so much fun!" I said.

Dr. Singh gave me that look again, the one that said "I told you so," but I didn't care. So what if she saw me having fun at Camp Newton. *I was having fun at Camp Newton!* I didn't care anymore who knew it.

"So, Dr. Singh," I said quickly. "How about those canoes?"

Riya and Sam laughed. I knew they would.

"And Sunny," I said, turning to my little sister. "Thanks for the great idea."

"What idea?" she asked, not looking up from her notebook.

AD INFINITUM!

I dove for the rock that Sam "planted" in the lake using a waterproof GPS device. Sam and I had Location Technology together, and Mr. Hunter let us borrow the GPS to play the game every day this week. Sam would hide the rock someplace in the lake and then give me the coordinates. Then I'd have to figure out where in the lake the rock was and dive for it. And then it was my turn to hide the rock. Science was fun when you took it outside.

Swimming to the bottom, I spotted it! I grabbed it from the sand and made for the surface, getting kicked in the head just as I came up. "Hey!" I said, spitting out a mouthful of water. But then I saw it was Junchao sputtering past me in an extremely splashy front crawl and smiled. I stuck my hand out of the water and gave Riya a thumbs-up. She was an excellent coach. It had taken Riya only five days of lessons and she just about had Junchao swimming. I hoped I could do the same thing for Camp Newton's softball team.

I had scheduled the first practice yesterday after dinner, but hardly anyone showed up. Junchao and Sam had worked through all the numbers and were building a list of what we should do and what we shouldn't do, but we needed kids to do anything. Tired of rock tracking, I splashed toward shore.

Sunny was sitting on the edge of the lake with a plastic bag. "What are you doing?"

"I'm building a water filtration system as part of one of my independent studies," she said. "Wanna help?"

"I guess all these independent studies are more important than my softball team?" I grumbled. Sunny was on the list of campers that had not shown up for softball practice last night.

"Without clean drinking water, everyone in the world would perish within three days," she said.

"Are you planning on drying up the world's water supply?" I asked. I said it as a joke, but when Sunny didn't answer right away, my heart gave a jump. "Well, are you?"

"You never know when you'll find yourself in a place without water," she said, concentrating on her plastic bag filled with water, sand, and rocks.

"A place without water . . . like the desert?"

She looked up at me from the edge of the sandy lake. "Yes, Masha, like the desert."

"Dad is supposed to pick us up here at camp, right?" I asked.

She shrugged.

I took a deep breath and went to hunt down my beach towel. Sunny Sweet couldn't possibly get us to the Sahara Desert, could she? She couldn't. Dr. Singh blew the whistle. It was time to head back to the labs and to Location Technology. Boo-hoo.

It's not that I hated Location Tech class like I did my enzyme class, but I guess I thought we'd be drawing treasure maps, and it turns out that we just talk about satellites. I started up the hill to our cabin to change. Dr. Singh walked up with me. "So, Masha, how is it going?"

I thought about pretending that I still hated camp, but it was kind of useless because I knew that she was just watching me in the water laughing so hard with Sam that I about swallowed the lake.

"I like it," I said, and then watched her smile. "But . . ."

"But?" she asked.

"I really want this softball game to work out, and no one came out for our first practice."

"Hmm," she said. "Maybe we need to create some incentive to play."

"What's incentive?"

"It's giving the campers a reason to play," she said. "Let me think. Well, the higher-level engineering and robotics classes are on their fluid dynamics section right now where they're building robots that can navigate underwater."

"How can robots help me get the kids to want to

play softball? Do we let them use the water robots to swing the bats?"

"No," laughed Dr. Singh, "but that's not a bad idea for next year. I was thinking that we'd take the canoes out using their robots. Anyone who wants to go on a robot canoe trip also has to show up for softball practice."

"You're brilliant, Dr. Singh!" I shouted, hugging her.

"So I've been told many times." She smiled.

"Oh, and Dr. Singh?"

"Yes, Masha."

"My dad said he was picking us up from camp, right? Sunny and I aren't getting on another plane by ourselves, are we?" I couldn't get the Sahara Desert off my mind.

Whenever Sunny got weirdly into something it made me nervous. I needed to stay on my toes or I'd find myself on the back of a camel somewhere.

"Yes, Masha, your dad is picking you up here at camp," she said.

Canoeing sounded so fun all on its own. But canoeing with robots sounded even more fun! And I wasn't alone in thinking this. Everybody at Camp Newton showed up two days later for our first robot canoe trip. Everybody but Sunny, that is.

Sunny told Dr. Singh that she had rhinopharyngitis, which sounded totally made up to me. But Dr. Singh looked worried and made her go back to the cabin to rest. I asked Sunny if she wanted me to stay with her, even though I completely didn't want to. She just asked me why. So I shrugged and ran. When the choice is between a robot canoe ride and sitting in the cabin . . . it's hard not to choose the robot canoe ride! Although the robots looked less like robots and more like a jumble of white pipes and wires with faces drawn on the front of them with black marker, but who cared, we were going canoeing!

"Do we have to wear these bright-orange vests?" complained Riya.

"Yes," Dr. Singh said. "And Molly and the rest of the counselors are in charge." To Molly she added, "You know what we talked about . . . approximately one kilometer out and back again."

"Yes, sir!" shouted Molly, her braids shaking from the force of her loud voice.

"You don't have to do that, Molly." Dr. Singh smiled.

"Yes, sir!" Molly repeated. And then to us she yelled, "Man the boats. Three to a vessel. Look alive!"

"I think Molly is going pirate on us," whispered Riya as she hopped in the boat with Molly. "Come on, Rachel, come with us," Riya said. "And bring your robot." Rachel was the girl with the pen around her neck, which I since learned wasn't a pen. It just looked like one. It was actually a tube with medicine in it with a needle on one end. You pulled off the cap over the needle and gave yourself a shot of the medicine if you were allergic to bees (which Rachel was) and a bee stung you. Rachel showed us how it worked the other night over dinner. A bee didn't even sting her, but she pulled out her pen and gave herself the shot! It was awesometastic! Although Dr. Singh didn't think so. She said you weren't supposed to fool around with that stuff. It was a weird thing to say because all we do here at Camp Newton is fool around with stuff that looks like it shouldn't be fooled around with. Rachel scrambled into the front of the boat with her robot and its remote control. Sam and I climbed into the canoe next to them and yelled for Junchao to join us with her robot.

Junchao went to step in, but then leaped into the air with a scream and went running from the canoe.

I looked down. "It's just a little spider, Junchao."

Picking up a leaf, I scooped the little guy out of the canoe and placed it on the sandy beach, where it scurried away. "It's now safer in the canoe than it is out here on the beach," I called to Junchao, and she leaped back into the canoe with her robot.

We were off.

We had paddles, but we didn't need them. The water robots pulled us along. Rachel and her robot slowly led us out into the lake since she had Molly in her boat. I sat and watched the shoreline move farther and farther away. We were leaving land. I sucked in a big, long breath to slow down my beating heart. It felt so cool to be bobbing through the water. Fun but scary at the same time. I turned and grinned at Sam. He smiled back at me, the lenses of his glasses sparkling in the sun. When I turned around to face the front of the boat, the canoe rocked back and forth in the water and my stomach did a little flip. These things seemed very "tippy."

At first I thought the robots would eventually speed up and plow us at warp speed across the lake, but we actually kind of puttered through the water. Not that I minded, it was just great to be in the boat. We were all pretty quiet. So quiet that we could hear the soft whirring of the underwater robots. Maybe I wasn't the only one who had never been in a canoe before.

"I just calculated our speed at approximately 2.2 knots," Sam called out.

"That's only two miles an hour," someone groaned.

"It's closer to two and a half," Junchao yelled back.

That did it. Everyone began to talk and laugh. "Hey, Masha!" Riya yelled, waving over at me. I waved back. Then I squinted my eyes and let the bright orange of our vests mix with the blue of the water and the yellow of the sun and the sound of everyone chattering away until it made me want to shout with happiness. We looked and sounded like a plain old group of camp kids, except for the fact that we were being pulled along through the water by robots! That is . . . until we turned the corner in the lake and saw another group of kids in canoes *not* being pulled along through the water by robots. And then the quiet was back. All you could hear were the soft chirping of frogs and the whirring of the little robot motors.

But then the other group of kids in canoes across the lake saw us, and the silence was broken. "Hey," one of them shouted, his voice echoing across the top of the water. "Look who it is! Camp Stupid."

They all laughed.

None of us did . . . mostly I think because we were

busy trying to understand the connection between the word "stupid" and "Newton." It didn't rhyme and we were a science and math camp, both of which have never been thought of as stupid. Anyway, the campers from Falcon Hill didn't seem to care that we were confused by their joke. They began paddling toward us.

It took us a second or two to react, but Junchao and Rachel and the others in control of the robots began to turn us around. You couldn't hear the soft whirring of the robots . . . just the splashing of Falcon Hill's oars as they headed toward us.

The oars!

"Use the oars," I yelled back at Sam. And then I yelled it to everyone, "USE YOUR OARS!" I held mine up over my head and shook it for all of Camp Newton to see. And then I put it in the water.

Paddling was a lot harder than it looked. I would dip my oar in too deep and not be able to even pull it back, or dip it in too little and almost fall flat on my back in the canoe. Sam kept sticking his oar into the water at the same time I would be pulling back on my oar, turning us in a circle so we had a great view of how fast the Falcon Hill camp was approaching. Rachel, Riya, and Molly crashed into us. And then the twins, James and Jason, in the canoe with Einstein (his name was really Einstein) bumped into the two of us. The rest of Camp Newton followed. In about a minute, we were surrounded by Falcon Hill kids. I could hear them laughing, but I couldn't see anything

through the spray of water they were sending our way with their oars. Molly tried to shout at them, but all you could hear was military-like gurgling. Then I did see something . . . a kid pulling Rachel's robot out of the water by its line. He whipped it into the air and around his head like a lasso and then sent it flying off into the lake. Before I could scream "No!" the Falcon Hill kids were dragging all the robots out of the water and throwing them out into the lake. Junchao jumped up to save her robot.

I was in the water so fast that I can't even remember falling overboard. My first idea was to get air. My second was to get Junchao. I found her bobbing in her orange jacket a little ways off from the cluster of kids. Sam swam over to us. "You guys okay?" I shook my head yes even though I wasn't sure if we were. I could hear Molly shouting at the Falcon Hill kids to cease and desist. But they weren't doing either of those things.

Once we were all completely soaked, from their splashes or from floating in the water, and the robots were all gone, the Falcon Hill kids got bored and paddled away.

"Anyone broken?" Molly called out. No one answered. "I meant hurt. Is anyone hurt?" There were some groans and a few nos. Molly told us all to sit tight while she did a head count. We were all there. "Okay, move out!"

Sam grabbed one of Junchao's arms and I grabbed the other, and we swam back to the canoe. The three of us held onto the side of the canoe while the others took turns pulling us back to shore. It was too hard to try to climb back into the boat.

The trip back was completely silent, except for the splashing of the oars in the lake. We hauled ourselves and the canoes back onto the beach and then, like a horde of sopping-wet zombies, we made our way to our cabins.

Sunny was lying on *my* bunk and scribbling in her notebook. I guess her rhino fever had gotten better. "What happened?"

"Why are your muddy feet all over my bunk? And why are your feet muddy anyway?" I asked. "I thought you were sick."

"I feel better," she said. "So why are you all wet?"

"Camp Falcon Hill," I grumbled, pulling off my soaked T-shirt and shorts. My stomach ached. Probably from swallowing a ton of lake water filled with algae. I pictured little algae swimming around in my belly, and my stomach hurt worse. "So now I guess the whole softball thing is over, right?"

"Why?" asked Riya.

"Because no one will want to sign up to go against the Falcon Hill kids after what just happened," I said.

"I want to!" said Riya, shoving her feet in her sneakers and picking up her softball mitt.

"I want to too," said Junchao, but looking more like she really didn't want to.

"Me too," I said, smiling at my two *gui mi*s. And then I pictured what I must have looked like flying overboard into the lake and I *really* wanted to! "I know," I said. "Let's think us up a sciencey battle cry. You know, like something we can yell when we get that run."

"There is no yelling in science," Sunny said, closing her notebook.

"How about *ad infinitum*?" suggested Riya. "It

127

translates as 'forevermore' in Latin, but it really means 'limitless.'"

"Perfect!" I laughed. "Even though our goal is to get one run, which kind of sounds like a limit. But those kids from Falcon Hill won't know it. *AD INFI-NITUM!*" I yelled.

"*AD INFINITUM!*" Junchao and Riya chanted together.

"Why did they call us Camp Stupid, anyway?" asked Junchao. Her long black hair was a huge mess from her drying it with a beach towel.

"I know," said Riya. "It doesn't even rhyme."

"And we were the ones using machines to propel us through the water while they had to rely on manual labor," I said. "OMG, I am totally becoming one of you!"

Riya, Junchao, and I broke down into giggles.

"I'm going to the lab," Sunny said.

Zero . . . the Lowest Point or Degree

We'd been practicing for four days straight, and things had been going fantastic. Sam and Junchao figured out that we needed to focus on throwing the ball, catching the ball, and not swinging at pitches that were not strikes. Basically we needed to learn how to play softball. Riya and I had stayed up late a few nights googling softball fundamentals on Dr. Singh's laptop. I read them out loud, and Riya took notes. Together with Sam and Junchao's statistics, we were slowly putting it all into action.

When I looked out over the field at Camp Newton's

softball team, I couldn't keep from smiling. *"Ad infinitum,"* I whispered under my breath. But my sciencey battle cry made me think of science, which made me think of Sunny Sweet—the only camper at Camp Newton not attempting to throw, hit, or catch a ball right now. This really could have hurt my good mood, but then I heard the crack of ball hitting bat and watched Riya send one flying. Those stats were right. *She really could hit the ball.* But she could also run and throw and catch and do just about anything good out there on the field.

"GO, RIYA!" Sam shouted and clapped as Riya ran the bases and little Einstein Mayer ran and ran and ran after the softball that had skipped off into the pine trees.

I walked over to Junchao and Sam. They were sitting in the bleachers. Junchao was hunched over her laptop. "Who's up next?" I asked.

"Well," said Junchao, "after spending time transforming all the numbers from an incomprehensible mass into a sequence in which the offense would take their turns at bat in the most optimal way . . ."

"Yeah, okay," I said. "Just tell me who's up?"

"That would be Rachel," said Sam.

"Rachel," I yelled. "You're up."

Rachel jumped up off the grass and ran for the bat, her EpiPen swinging around her neck on a chain.

"Do you want me to hold your bee pen?" I asked. I knew it was an EpiPen, but I liked my name for it better.

"Nah," she said. "It won't bother me."

Just then I spotted Sunny walking past the softball field and toward the woods, wearing a strange green-and-brown outfit. She had mud smeared all over her face and didn't look as skinny as usual.

"What are you doing?"

"Camo testing," she said. And she kept walking.

"What?"

"I'm testing out camouflage outfits," she said louder as she made her way past me.

"Why are you so puffy?" I called after her.

"I'm wearing several layers of polypropylene thermal underwear," she yelled back over her shoulder.

I almost asked why but then stopped myself. You could ask Sunny questions forever and a day, but you never got the answer you were looking for. I watched Sunny Sweet march off in her poppyseed underwear looking like a dirty marshmallow and just shrugged. Then I turned back to Rachel. "Batter up!" I shouted with a smile.

Junchao picked up a stack of papers from the bleacher bench, and then she threw them up into the air with a scream, leaping away from the bench and batting at her arms and legs and jumping in a twisty circle.

"Junchao, it's just a stupid bug," I said.

"That was a praying mantis, and they aren't stupid," said Sam. "The mantis is considered a god in some African cultures."

"Really?" Junchao asked. "A god?"

"Are we here to play ball or what?" I grumbled, happy with how much I sounded like a real coach.

Sam picked up Junchao's papers and inspected them, and then he handed them back to her. Junchao began reading out a list of numbers to Rachel. "There were 146 pitches thrown in the game last year, with 58 of those judged to be balls by the umpire. This gives us approximately a 40 percent chance of the pitch being called a ball. Also, it is likely that many of the pitches swung at were also balls. I've calculated your batting average at .164, so . . ."

"Come on," James yelled from the pitching mound.

"So," continued Junchao, "with fifteen at bats you've hit the ball . . ."

All I heard was *blah, blah, blah.*

"Therefore," finished Junchao, "with numbers such as these, it becomes obvious what you need to do."

Rachel blew a big bubble with her chewing gum and let it smack to a pop. We looked at one another. And then we looked at Sam.

"Just stand there, Rachel," Sam explained. "Don't try to hit the ball. Go for the walk."

"Got it," said Rachel, stepping up to home plate.

James pitched. Rachel stood. James pitched. Rachel stood. James pitched. Rachel stood. James pitched. Rachel giggled as the fourth pitch was announced a ball and then she was off and running to first base. All along the sidelines, Camp Newton cheered!

This was so fun.

That night when I climbed into my bunk, I dreamed of catcher's mitts and home runs and spitting sunflower seeds onto the floor of the dugout and that fantastic clinking sound of ball meeting bat and of a bright-blue sky and green, green grass and white toilet paper . . . white toilet paper?

I sat up . . . into a line of toilet paper strung across

my bunk. Tearing it down, I looked around. There was toilet paper everywhere! What the heck?

I jumped out of my bed and ran to the door of our cabin. When I opened the door I was met by a wall of toilet paper. I tore it down, only to discover that the entire world was covered in soft white paper. It hung from trees. It wrapped itself around every bush. It clung to the other cabins. It ran along the stone paths. It was everywhere, like a strange white vine that had twisted itself into and around all of Camp Newton.

"Molly!" I screamed.

I heard the thud as her feet hit the cabin floor. And then I heard a few muffled bad words. I guess toilet paper had crawled into her cabin as well. Her door swung open. Now I heard the bad words loud and clear.

There was scraping and exclaiming behind me as Riya, Sunny, and Junchao jumped out of bed. Other cabin doors swung open, along with mouths, as Camp Newton discovered it had been . . .

"T-P'd," said Dr. Singh. "That's what Mr. Johnson from Falcon Hill called it."

We all stood in a group surrounding Dr. Singh outside the mess hall door, which had been spray-painted with the sentence We will wipe our butts with you at the game.

"Why did they do it?" Jason asked.

Dr. Singh took a big breath. "Mr. Johnson said it was just a fun prank, that his campers didn't mean anything by it."

"Will they clean it up?" asked Jason's twin brother, James.

Dr. Singh said that she didn't think so. And that we'd all have breakfast and attend our labs, and then we'd do it ourselves.

"That's going to cut into softball practice," I complained.

Dr. Singh just shook her head and gave a little shrug.

"I don't think I want to play softball anymore," whispered Rachel.

"What?" I said.

"Me neither," said James.

There were a bunch of *me neithers* that followed.

My heart ached. "It's just toilet paper," I said. "Remember the canoe trip and our robots!"

But instead of everyone getting excited like they did before, there were just long faces and nods as they remembered.

"Let's get going with our day. Things will look brighter after breakfast," Dr. Singh said.

It was the first time that Dr. Singh had been wrong. Things didn't look brighter, not after breakfast, and not after labs, and not after dinner. No one showed up to practice that afternoon after we cleaned up the toilet paper . . . or the next afternoon . . . or the next. Dr. Singh said to give everyone time. But we didn't have much time left. There were only two days until the game.

Junchao and Riya tried to get my mind off of softball. Riya showed me everything she loved about engineering, which seemed mostly just steam trains. Riya really loved steam trains. I even sat through her favorite movie in the rec room, which was this really long video about steam trains in India.

Junchao tried to help me too. She became the bug whisperer . . . befriending every single living thing that had a bunch of legs. She even started naming them, although keeping the names of the ants straight was really hard, so in honor of me, she named all of them Masha. It was a little strange because everybody in camp starting calling ants Masha. So you'd hear, "Don't step on Masha." Or "Masha was crawling up my wall last night." They were my *gui mis*, and I loved that they were trying to help, but I didn't stop thinking about the softball game.

For the first time in almost three weeks, I missed my mom and Mrs. Song and Alice and my own bed and food made out of stuff I'd heard of. I just wanted to go home. It was like Falcon Hill had toilet papered my heart. Before being T-P'd, the big game was about my coaching, and Sam and Junchao's statistics, and Riya's batting, and getting that run for Camp Newton. After being T-P'd, it became about Falcon Hill. All I could see were those kids in their canoes, with their faces twisted up laughing at us. I guess everybody at Camp Newton felt the same. Maybe it was better to just show up to the game and take down statistics and get it over with. But it didn't feel better.

We all went to our classes and labs and meals, but none of us bothered Dr. Singh about swimming anymore. And I didn't bother anyone about softball anymore. And no one seemed that happy anymore.

Even Sunny, who hadn't taken off her lab coat or pulled her nose out of her notebook since we arrived at camp, tried to cheer me up. She met me outside of Urban Landscapes class with what looked like a fur pouch thrown over her shoulder and a big stick in her hand. "Do you want to join me in my independent study on primitive living skills?" She asked.

I could totally see that she didn't really want me to.

"No," I said.

And Sunny skipped off toward the woods.

Okay, no one seemed that happy anymore except for Sunny Sweet.

Long Division

It was the day of the big game, and we were having buckwheat porridge for breakfast. I didn't even know that porridge was real! I thought it was something they ate only in fairy tales. And weirdly, it sounded good when they ate it in stories . . . hot and delicious. In real life, it's just hot. Anyway, buckwheat porridge was enough to ruin anyone's day, even without the fact that Camp Falcon Hill was going to wipe their butts with us today.

"*Ni mei shi ba?*" Junchao asked, putting her hand on my shoulder. A lot of times I didn't know the meanings of the words when Junchao spoke to me in Chinese, but the longer I knew her, the more I felt the meanings.

"I'm okay," I lied.

Junchao, Sam, and Riya went back to chatting and eating gross buckwheat porridge. I mixed my buckwheat around in my bowl and thought about my dad. He would be here in one day and a wake-up. That's how Molly taught me to count days. She said not to add in the last one, but call it "a wake-up" instead. It's military slang. Molly says that when you're waiting for something to happen, saying it this way makes it sound closer. And so my dad would be here in one day and a wake-up.

Sunny came late, got her porridge, and sat down with us at the table.

"It sure took you forever to get ready this morning," I said. "I can't believe Molly didn't make you drop and give her fifty push-ups."

"She did," said Sunny. "But I could do only two."

I noticed Junchao fiddling with a box on her lap.

"What is that?" I asked. "Something to eat?"

I was pretty hungry and anything would be better than this porridge.

"Oh," Junchao said, putting the box on the table and opening it up. "Meet Ronald," she said, introducing us to a little green grasshopper.

"That is not something to eat." I sighed. Junchao was really going overboard with the bug love.

"Grasshoppers are actually very nutritious," Sunny said, with her mouth full of buckwheat. "There are like twenty grams of protein per grasshopper. You just pluck off their legs and wings and roast them. You can't eat them raw because of external parasites."

Junchao quickly put the top of the box back on Ronald and put it down on her lap. The rest of us just ignored Sunny's gross little cooking lesson.

"Maybe we'll get a run at the game today anyway," said Sam. He dipped his spoon into my porridge. I pushed the bowl over to him. Buckwheat was definitely better than roasted grasshoppers, but I still wasn't eating it.

"That's right," Junchao said. "It could happen."

"What are the odds of that?" I said.

Sunny opened her mouth to answer, but I cut her off. "No one cares about the game anymore."

"Falcon Hill seemed to care," Riya said.

"Yeah," said Sam. "Although they never cared about it before."

"They didn't?" I asked.

"Not before the game anyway," he said. "They showed up that day all pumped up and ready to squash us. But they never cared enough to send us messages painted on doors."

"That's weird," I said.

"That is weird," Riya added. "It's like they knew we were practicing."

Sunny coughed.

We all looked over at her.

"Rhinopharyngitis," she said.

"Sunny," I said.

She squirmed in her seat. "What?" she asked.

"Tell me."

She blinked at me.

"Now!"

"Well, I didn't want to tell those guys you were practicing," she said. "They made me."

"What?" I said.

"I was dowsing for water up on the camp's west trail when I bumped into them in the woods. They were on a hike."

"What's dowsing?" Junchao asked.

"We don't care," I said. "We only care about what you told them."

"It's a technique for searching for water that is underground," Sunny said quickly.

I growled at her. "Just tell us the part where you told on us!"

"They said they'd break my divining rod, Masha," she whined. "And it took me three days to find a forked stick of hickory!"

"So you told them we were practicing?" I said. My voice was so high pitched that it hurt my own ears.

"Masha," Riya said. I knew she was warning me to calm down, but I so was *not* calming down.

"I had to, Masha," Sunny said. "One of the girls

said that if I didn't tell them something they didn't know, they'd break my stick. First I told them that the universe was expanding. I thought for sure that they didn't know that. But then they changed the rules. They said that it had to be something about our camp. So I told them that our labs were hooked into the LIS system, and they didn't like that. Then I told them that we just installed a robotic pipetting station to help in the sequencing of our DNA fragments, and *then they were really going to break my stick*! When I told them about you guys practicing softball, I couldn't believe it, but they just handed my stick right back to me." She shrugged. "Weird, right?"

"You," I said.

"What?" she asked.

"Masha," Riya repeated.

But I lost it. "All I wanted was that one run. I didn't even want to be here. You made me come here!" I shouted. "I could have been at the Lone Creek Dude Ranch riding my horse right this minute."

"But Masha," Sunny said. "The surprise . . ."

"I don't care about the surprise anymore," I shouted.

"And I don't care about you! I wish that you had just gotten lost back at the airport in Boston!"

Sunny's eyes got big. And then she jumped up from the table and ran out of the mess hall.

No one moved. No one said a word. And then Ronald chirped in his box and broke the ice.

"Masha," Riya said. "Those Falcon Hill campers are bullies. Sunny didn't . . ."

"I know," I interrupted. I got up from the table and ran after my little sister.

The sun was so bright, and when it mixed with the tears filling my eyes it stung. I knew it wasn't really Sunny's fault, but it still felt like her fault deep inside me. Why did all the bad things that happened to me have Sunny's name all over them? I ran to the cabin and threw open the door. Sunny wasn't there. I was just about to turn around and try the labs when I noticed something. Or rather, I noticed nothing. Sunny's things were gone. And my things were gone too. Our shelves were completely empty! I ran over to them to get a closer look. Who would have taken all our stuff? Falcon Hill? But then I remembered what I'd just shouted at Sunny, that I wished she'd gotten lost. So did she run back here and take all our stuff and leave? That fast? Or . . . had she been planning to leave? I remembered Sunny coming into breakfast late. All of a sudden I pictured Sunny in my mind: all hunched over her little notebook, and walking by the softball field in those silly dirty-marshmallow clothes, and building fires, and making clean water, and learning about weather, and staying behind from the canoe trip, and having those muddy shoes, and all the other million things that Sunny was doing here at camp that I hadn't noticed before. And I knew that Sunny Sweet had been planning this. But why?

Ugh, that question!

I threw myself onto my bunk, folding my arms across my chest and putting one ankle over the other in a position of so not caring that Sunny Sweet had gotten herself lost . . . again! I'm sure that she was probably up there in the woods in some awesome fort she built, watching the Discovery Channel on satellite television, munching on roasted grasshoppers, and totally laughing at me. Well she could laugh right through ten snowstorms this winter for all I cared. We weren't a binary relationship, we were a long-division relationship, and I was dividing Sunny right out of my life.

I lay there for a minute. And then another. But in the middle of the third minute I hopped off the bunk.

Sunny. She was right. She was always right. We were this stupid binary thing she talked about. Even though I wanted to drop-kick her across the entire state of Maine, I couldn't let her get lost out in it. I had to find her. I looked for a pencil and paper to write Riya and Junchao a note to tell them where I'd gone.

Where was I going?

All I could think of was heading off into the woods where I saw her walk that day during practice. I found a pencil next to Junchao's journal. But I didn't want to open her journal to get a piece of paper because a journal is private. I looked around the cabin for something else to write on and spotted Sunny's little notebook lying half under my bunk. I walked over and grabbed it off the floor. I opened it up to the first page and there they were . . . GPS coordinates N43 39.6921 W70 15.31955, the numbers that would lead me to my little sister.

Canada, Oh Canada

I ran to my Location Technology class and borrowed a GPS from Mr. Hunter's lab. He always lets us. Using the GPS, I figured out pretty quickly exactly where Sunny was. According to my calculations, it was only a twenty-minute walk into the woods. And I loved thinking those words, *according to my calculations*. They made me smile. But then I remembered the softball game, and my heart fell.

I had about an hour and a half until the game, so I didn't have to hurry. I started into the woods right where I saw her the day she had on the dirty-marshmallow outfit. You had to walk across the softball field to get to the trail that led into the woods. We hadn't done any hiking at camp, but it was on my wish list of activities I was making Dr. Singh for next summer.

Next summer . . . I thought about Junchao and Riya and Sam and smiled as I ducked under a low pine branch and into the shade of the trail that led into the woods. The ground was soft with needles. The air was cool on my face. The birds chirped. The sun slipped through the pines and landed on the forest floor, making little puddles of light. I remembered seeing Camp Newton for the first time that night we drove into the clearing in Poly. The camp in my memory is so different than the one I know now. That camp was distant and strange, and the smell of the air made me feel like we'd landed on another planet. The camp I know is familiar and happy, even if Falcon Hill ruined my softball game. And next year, after a year of practice with my softball team at school, who knows what I could teach everyone when I got back here.

After a little bit of walking, I turned a corner in the trail and there was a bright-orange backpack hanging in a tree with Sunny standing next to it, wearing the other one. It had taken me less than an hour to find my little sister. *Not bad, Masha Sweet,* I told myself.

Sunny spotted me right away. "Masha!" she shouted. And then she turned around and started to run.

"Sunny, wait!" I took off after her.

She scurried down a hill and behind a clump of pine trees. I ran after her.

I was a lot faster than Sunny, but she kept making crazy zigzaggy turns in the woods and diving low under pine branches. If it weren't for that bright-orange backpack, I'd have lost her a bunch of times.

"Sunny!" I kept calling. "Stop!"

But she wouldn't listen. She just kept bouncing away from me around a tree or down a hill. Each time I'd catch a streak of orange up ahead of me and I'd race toward it. At first, I couldn't wait to get my hands on her skinny little neck for running away from me, but as she kept running and running, I started to get scared. She disappeared into a clump of trees. And then I spotted her running up and over a ridge to my left. She was getting farther away from me.

"Sunny," I called. "Sunny, I'm sorry. I'm sorry that I yelled at you." I thought I saw an orange speck in the distance stop. "Sunny, I'm glad you brought me to Camp Newton. You're right. I like it here. Actually, I kind of love it here. And I never would have come if it weren't for you." The orange speck began to move toward me, and in a minute, the speck became Sunny. She stood in front of me. Her cheeks were red from running and she was still breathing heavily. But she was listening to me.

"I'm not mad about the dumb softball game, and I'm not mad that you brought me here, and I'm not mad about Daddy's surprise anymore. I'm just happy that you came back."

I walked over and gave her a hug, my arms squishing the orange backpack and Sunny together. "You know what else I'm happy about? I'm happy that you picked out these neon bright-orange backpacks because I never would have been able to keep up with you if you hadn't been wearing it. Wearing orange is a mistake if you're trying to get lost."

A mistake.

Sunny didn't make mistakes. I slowly let go and backed away from her. I had been set up. She wasn't hiding. She had been running with that orange backpack for a reason. She left me those GPS coordinates

in her book. I was supposed to be here. How did she do this to me every time?

"Masha," she said.

I looked around. I had no idea where we were. "Sunny, what did you do?" I growled.

"Don't worry. I planned everything," she said.

"That is exactly why I am totally worried!" I shouted.

I turned around and walked away.

"Is that the way back to camp?" Sunny asked.

"Is it?" I snapped.

She shrugged.

"Sunny Sweet, you are so going to get us un-lost right this minute. Why, Sunny? Why would you get us lost? Why didn't you just get *you* lost?"

"Without you?" she asked.

"Yes, without me!" I shouted.

"But," she said, looking confused. It was weird to see Sunny look confused. "I don't do anything without you. You're my sister." I saw her eyes glow with tears.

I hated when she did that, made me feel bad when she was doing something crazy like getting us lost in the woods. I stomped off into the trees. I didn't care anymore which way camp was. I just wanted to be far away from my sister.

Sunny followed. "Masha, we can go to Canada. I have it all planned. It's a long walk—maybe a couple of weeks. And there might be a mountain or two. But they're not like the Rockies or anything up here."

I stopped. "Canada? What are you talking about?"

"Did you know that the police in Canada all ride horses, Masha? They're called Mounties. Really their full name is the Royal Canadian Mounted Police. And you can be one . . . when you turn nineteen. You'll probably have to learn French and pledge allegiance to Canada too, but by then we'll love living up there."

I stopped and swung around to face her. "Sunny!" I shouted. "Stop talking."

She stopped.

Okay, now I had to remember how Dr. Singh got Sunny to answer that question in the airport. I think I remember. I think it was that she asked a question that could only be answered with a yes or a no. "Sunny," I said, looking right into her eyes. And then I lost it.

"WHY ARE WE RUNNING AROUND OUT HERE IN THE WOODS AND TALKING ABOUT CLIMBING MOUNTAINS AND SAYING THE PLEDGE OF ALLEGIANCE IN FRENCH AND BECOMING CANADIAN POLICE ON HORSES?"

That wasn't a yes or no question. And Sunny just blinked at me for a second. Tiny tears dripped out of her eyes. And in that second I understood. "This doesn't have anything to do with the softball game and Camp Newton, does it?"

Sunny shook her head no.

"This is about Daddy's surprise, isn't it?"

She shook her head yes.

"You know what the surprise is, don't you?"

She shook her head yes.

"Am I going to like it?"

Sunny looked at me for a second. And then she slowly shook her head no. As she did, more tears popped into her eyes and started down her cheeks.

"Sunny," I said. "I don't care about a horse anymore. I really don't. We couldn't have put a horse in our backyard anyway. It's way too small. And he'd probably wander into Mrs. Song's yard and eat all her lilac bushes and you know how much Mrs. Song loves her lilac bushes."

"It's a person," Sunny choked through her tears. "The surprise is a person."

"Daddy is giving us a person?"

"A girlfriend person," she spit through her tears.

"A girlfriend person?" I repeated. "A girlfriend person?" And then I got it. A girlfriend person. The surprise was that Daddy had a girlfriend.

I sat down hard onto the pine needles. A girlfriend person? Girlfriends were something teenagers had, not dads. Was my dad even allowed to have a girlfriend? My stomach felt like a giant black bruise. I wanted Sunny to stop crying. Each time she sobbed it was like a punch in my sore stomach. I looked around. Nothing looked right, the pine trees, the sky, even my sneakers. They looked too bright and too close to me. I wanted to push it all back to where it belonged.

"You see, Masha. We have to go to Canada," Sunny said, gulping down a big pile of tears.

"You've known the whole time, haven't you?" My

voice had a hard time getting out, so it sounded like I was whispering. "Because you were pretending to be mom. So when Dr. Singh said that night in the mess hall that Mommy didn't like the surprise, that was really you."

She shook her head yes. And then I started to cry, which was a huge mistake because Sunny jumped right on top of me as if she could smother my sadness like a fire. Her elbow jabbed into my chest and her knobby knee was crushing my leg. But strangely, it worked. Her skinny little body thrown on top of me did smother my sadness. Or maybe I just needed her to get off me. I stopped crying, and Sunny sat down next to me.

"I'm sorry," I said. "I'm sorry that you knew this horrible thing for so long and all I cared about was a stupid horse."

"That's okay, Masha. We'll just go to Canada. You and me."

I didn't say anything for a minute. And then I didn't say anything for another minute.

"Masha?"

"Sunny," I said.

"No," she said. "We have to go."

"Sunny, we can't."

"Yes, we can, Masha. I have a whole plan. I know everything . . . how to skin animals and cook them, how to build shelters when it gets cold, how to plant stuff that will grow in cold weather, how to make shoes out of tree bark, how to . . ."

"What about Mommy?"

She squished her little lips together and looked at me. "I wanted her to come too, Masha, but I didn't know how to get her to camp. And then when Babushka broke her hip, I had to come up with a whole new plan."

"We can't leave Mommy, Sunny."

Her lips wiggled. "I just want to go h . . . ," she said. And then tried again. "I just want to go h . . ."

I took her hand and squeezed it. "I just want to go home too."

We sat together in the pine needles for a long time. I thought about the girlfriend. I tried to picture her, but she was just this fuzzy idea in my head without a face. It was hard to think about my dad without my mom. I could think about my mom without my dad because that's how it's been. But my dad without my mom? We just hadn't spent that much time with my dad since they got divorced. And my dad . . . with another lady?

Off in the distance there was a *clonk*—that fantastic sound of ball meeting bat. It was followed by the faint *aahing* of a crowd. The softball game had started.

A Little Bingo

Sunny and I sat and listened to the game. There were a lot of *clonks* and a lot of *aahs*. And we both knew that the sounds were not coming from Camp Newton.

"We probably wouldn't have gotten that run anyway." I sighed.

"Of course you could," Sunny said, "if Falcon Hill would let you out of the set line-up rule. Cal McConnell is your HBP leader, which is the hit by pitch leader. He gets on first. Einstein is your smallest player and the most likely to be walked. The numbers look good for a walk following an HBP batter since the pitcher is nervous. Cal McConnell is on second. Einstein is on first. When it comes to connecting to the ball, Rachel is second to Riya and is your next batter. She can't hit far, but she's left-handed, making it likely to hit the ball toward first base. They will get her out, and most likely Einstein too, in a double play. But Cal should be able to make it to third. You'll need Riya up next. She's your only statistical hope of bringing Cal back to home plate."

I stared at Sunny.

"I was watching from Dr. Singh's office. I also went through the files. Truthfully, Camp Newton wasn't as challenging a science camp as I hoped, and I had spare time."

I jumped up from the pine needles. "Let's do it."

"Do what?"

"Do that, your plan."

"But my plan is Canada."

"Sunny," I said, looking down at her. "I don't want

to ride horses in Canada and learn the pledge of allegiance in French. I want to get that run, and I want to go home to Mom."

"But . . . Daddy."

"Yeah, I know."

I thought about Oscar/Charlie/Thunder/Black Cloud. I hadn't thought about him in almost three weeks. And now he had turned into a fuzzy lady that I didn't ever want to meet. "Sunny," I said. "Remember when we moved to the new house in New Jersey, and the bedrooms smelled like lemon cleaning soap, and we were scared of Mrs. Song because she didn't talk a lot, and we had to grocery shop at a ShopRite instead of a Stop & Shop like we always did?"

Sunny shook her head yes.

"Remember how that all felt wrong?"

Again, Sunny shook her head yes.

"And now the bedrooms just smell like our stuff, and Mrs. Song is our favorite person ever, and you know where every single thing is in the ShopRite and can even find it in less than thirty seconds!"

"Less than twenty-three seconds," Sunny said.

Clonk.

Aahhhhhhh.

I smiled at my little sister. "Twenty-three seconds, that is a pretty good record. So let's go set another good record. Let's go get a run for Camp Newton. Let's go wipe our butts with Falcon Hill," I said.

"Ewww!" Sunny laughed. But then she started running down the hill, the orange backpack bobbing about on her back. And I ran after her.

Sunny found her way back to the trail in a few minutes, and ten minutes after that, I could see the end of the trail up ahead. Sunny dashed out into the sunshine, but I held back a second. Falcon Hill was out there. I remembered their faces and shouts from the canoe trip. I tried to take a big breath, but my chest was so heavy that it wouldn't move to let the air in.

"Masha?" Sunny called.

"Coming." I gulped. But I wasn't.

Sunny's head peeked back under the pine branches. She blinked up at me where I stood.

"What if we don't get the run?" I asked. "What happens if your plan doesn't work?"

"In science," Sunny said, "we never say that an experiment failed. We say that we have now learned what doesn't work."

I laughed, and then I followed my little sister out into the sunshine.

The game was a mass of color in the distance, but as we got closer I could see that Falcon Hill was dressed completely in blue and white and that Camp Newton was a mix of our everyday colors. Dr. Singh was wearing a green sari and holding a bat in one hand and a clipboard in the other. Molly stood next to her in khakis and a black tank top, with all her braids tied up in a tight bun on the top of her head. They looked out of place on the softball field. I spotted Sam, Junchao, and Riya sitting in the bleachers, and one second later, they spotted me back. All three of their faces said the exact same thing as I headed toward them: *Where have you been?*

They clamored down the bleachers and met me alongside the route from home plate to first base. "Where have you been?" they asked all at once.

"Sorry," I said. "Sunny . . . lost some stuff up in the woods and I had to help her find it."

Sunny and I looked at each other and smiled.

"Well, you didn't miss anything," said Sam. "It's the sixth inning, and they're winning twenty-four to zero."

"Masha, Sunny," Dr. Singh called, "come get your assignments."

I walked over to Dr. Singh and Molly. She handed me a sheet with lots of boxes on it.

"Sorry we're late," I said.

Dr. Singh smiled at me. "I was worried," she said. "I thought that the disappointment of your first experiment not going as you'd hoped would sour you on the game."

"No experiment fails," I said, quoting my little sister. "It just teaches us what doesn't work."

Again Dr. Singh smiled. I was going to miss her smile. "Okay, girls, you two are going to focus on offensive stats."

"Actually, Dr. Singh," I interrupted, "Sunny and I have a plan."

"I was hoping that you did," she said.

"Molly, can you ask the umpire if it's okay if we change the batting lineup?" I asked.

"Got your 6!" Molly said, saluting. I didn't know exactly what Molly said, but I knew she was on it. Right before she turned to go, I noticed for the first time that Molly had a deep dimple in each of her cheeks.

Dr. Singh handed me the clipboard. "It's the bottom of the sixth inning. We're up. And we've got one out."

"Okay," I said, smiling.

"Oh, and girls, we only play six innings," she added.

"Okay," I said, no longer smiling.

She squeezed my shoulder. "Just go for it," she whispered.

"*Gui mi*s!" I shouted. And Junchao, Sam, and Riya came running.

"That's not how you say the plural," Junchao said.

"We don't have time for a Chinese lesson right now, Junchao. We need to get our run."

"Really?" asked Sam, glancing over at the campers of Camp Newton slumped in the stands over their statistics.

"Affirmative," shouted Molly from home plate. That I understood.

"Okay, here's the plan," I said. "We're just going to get one man on base. If we can do this, I think our guys will rally."

"Yup, that will work," said Riya. "So how are you going to do that?"

"Cal McConnell!" I shouted. And then I handed Sunny the clipboard. "Go to it, Coach Sweet."

Cal bent his head down to Sunny while she whispered in his ear. Falcon Hill's pitcher shielded his eyes from the sun with his mitt and glared over at us. Grouchy comments began to come from the blue-and-white side of the field: "Come on," and "We don't have all day," and "This game is so over." The Camp Newton campers looked up from their statistics, confused. Finally, Cal stood up and walked to home plate. Everyone watched Cal swing the bat up and behind his shoulder and crouch into batting position.

Falcon Hill pitched. Cal let the ball fly past him without moving. He stayed in position like a statue.

"Ball one," cried the umpire.

The second pitch came past Cal. He never moved. "Ball two," cried the umpire.

There was some loud grumbling heard from Falcon Hill's bleachers. The pitcher removed his hat and wiped the sweat from his forehead. And then he wound up and pitched. The ball flew up and over the umpire. Cal didn't move. The catcher did. He had to remove his mask and go find the ball.

"Ball three," cried the umpire.

The pitcher stomped his foot. And when the catcher threw him the ball, he missed it. The shortstop picked it up off the field and tossed it to the pitcher, who looked as if he was mumbling to himself.

Cal moved a tiny, tiny bit. He looked over at Sunny. Sunny gave him a thumbs-up. He looked back at the pitcher. The pitcher wound up but wobbled a bit in the middle of it. When the ball left his mitt, it traveled in a strange arc toward home plate. Cal didn't even wince. The ball hit him right above the elbow. "Take your base," yelled the umpire. A giant cheer went up in the Camp Newton stands.

"Ad infinitum!" I shouted.

Riya joined me. *"Ad infinitum!"* we shouted together.

And then all of Camp Newton joined in. We shouted for one straight minute and would have kept going but the umpire stood up and looked out at us through the fencing and drew a line across his neck with his pointer finger. We shut up.

"Batter up!" cried the umpire.

I looked over at Sunny. She was showing Einstein Google images on her phone of baseball players holding a bat. "Sunny," I yelled. "He needs to get out there." She said one last thing to Einstein, and he walked to home plate. He looked scared . . . mostly because his knees were really wobbly. When he got to home plate, he stuck out his hand to shake the umpire's hand. The umpire was confused, but he shook. Then he tried to shake the catcher's hand, but the Falcon Hill bleachers erupted with "Come on!" And so Einstein stood by home plate and raised the bat up behind his head. He was so tiny that the catcher was the same size as him, and the catcher was crouching down. The pitcher wound up to throw his pitch, and poor Einstein was shaking so hard that he was having trouble holding onto the bat.

The pitch came in two feet over Einstein's head. And so did the next. The third pitch rolled over home plate like the pitcher was at a bowling alley and not on a softball field. The fourth pitch was called a strike. Falcon Hill's bleachers screamed out in happiness.

Camp Newton's bleachers were silent. The fifth pitch flew over the plate. The umpire took a big breath and then yelled, "Strike two!"

The Falcon Hill campers jumped up from their seats and howled. The pitcher leaped into the air. Einstein dropped his bat and had to quickly scramble to pick it back up again. The catcher tossed the pitcher the ball, and the pitcher wound up to pitch with a big smile on his face. And then the ball left his hand, flew toward home plate, and popped the umpire right in his mask. "BALL FOUR!" cried the umpire.

Falcon Hill's bleachers exploded with boos until their counselors shushed them up. Camp Newton's bleachers didn't cheer, but instead huddled a little closer to each other. Einstein ran out to first base and tried to shake the first baseman's hand. The kid on first moved away from him. Einstein shrugged and then waved at Sunny. Sunny waved back. Then Sunny looked over at me and waved. I waved back. This was great!

There was one out. Cal was on second. Einstein

was on first. Rachel walked to home plate with her bee pen swinging around her neck. "She just needs to hit the ball," I whispered to myself. But Junchao heard me.

"*Ad infinitum,*" she whispered back without taking her eyes from home plate.

Rachel took a batter position and then leaped up into the air with a scream. "It stung me. It stung me," she cried.

Dr. Singh flew out to the plate, her sari a big blur of green. She sat Rachel on the ground at home plate. She helped Rachel take the bee pen from off her neck, open it, and . . .

"Ouch," Rachel said with a frown.

The umpire helped Rachel to her feet while Dr. Singh took out her cell phone. "Can I still bat?" Rachel asked.

"I'm calling an ambulance. You're going to the hospital to be checked out."

"So can I still bat?" she asked again.

"No!" said Dr. Singh. "You're sitting in the bleachers with me until it arrives." And then she announced to everyone that Rachel would be fine and that the game could continue.

Sunny tugged on my T-shirt sleeve.

"Riya?" I asked.

"You," she said.

"Me?" I asked.

"Yes. According to Sam's freshest statistics, you are the third most likely to connect with the ball," she said. "We need to save Riya for last."

"Me?" I asked.

"But you've got to hit the ball hard," Sunny said. "You don't run that fast. And if you hit it too softly, they'll be able to throw out Einstein and then throw you out. That would be three outs, and Cal wouldn't have given us the run."

"Me?" I asked.

Sunny handed me the helmet and the bat. "You," she said.

"BATTER UP!" the umpire yelled.

"Hit it *hard*," she said.

Home plate was only fifteen feet away from where

I'd been standing, but it felt like I'd entered a whole different world. In this world, there wasn't enough air to breathe and my eyes didn't work very well, but my ears worked especially well, and they heard all the horrible shouts of "strike her out" and "easy out" that came from the Falcon Hill bleachers. When the umpire shouted, "PLAY BALL," it sounded as if he'd yelled it inside of me. And when the pitcher wound up his pitch, I heard a *whoosh* and all sound was completely and totally gone. I watched the ball fly from the pitcher's hand. But that's all I watched, because after that, I closed my eyes and swung my bat.

I didn't hear the *clonk*. I felt it . . . right up through my elbows and into my shoulders. And then I heard the screams. "RUN!"

I headed for first base, running faster than I'd ever run in my whole life . . . faster even than I'd run after Sunny. I ran so fast that I ran right past first base and out into right field. I had no idea where I'd hit the ball or who was going after it or whether it was on its way to first base or whether it had already gotten there.

After I stopped running, the blood was pumping

through my head so hard that I couldn't hear what the first-base umpire said.

I did see his hand signal though, and I was out.

I walked to the sidelines. Everyone was cheering. Camp Falcon was cheering because I was out. Camp Newton was cheering because I'd moved Einstein to second base and Cal to third. Junchao, Sam, and Sunny ran over to me and hugged me tight. I was so happy that it was over. And I was so happy that I'd hit the ball. But there was a little piece of me that wasn't so happy about getting out, even if it didn't matter that I had. When the three of them let go, my knees were done holding me up and I slid down onto the grass. It was a perfect spot to watch Riya walk to home plate. She didn't need Sunny to tell her that she was up next.

Off in the distance, we heard the wail of Rachel's ambulance. Riya crouched low into position. Falcon Hill chanted at her, "Batter, batter, batter, batter," and the pitcher wound up to pitch. The ball hit the catcher's glove with a thud. "Steeerike one!" shouted the umpire.

Riya crouched again and twirled her bat in the air behind her head, signaling to the pitcher to pitch the ball. He did. "Steeerike two!" Falcon Hill was one out away from wiping their butts with Camp Newton for another year. My eyes welled up with tears, but I knew that if the next ball hit that catcher's glove that it was going to be all right, and that we didn't need that one run . . . that it wasn't even about that one run. It was about everything that had happened to get us here. I stared through my tears at Riya as the ambulance lights came into view at the top of the dirt road.

"Give us a little bingo, Riya!" shouted Dr. Singh.

I could see Riya's cheek widen in a smile under her helmet, and I watched her crouch just a tiny, tiny bit down farther.

The pitch rocketed toward Riya, and Riya sent it right back the other way so hard and so fast and so high that I got it confused with a bird flying over the game for a second. Both bleachers exploded in screams that you couldn't hear due to the ambulance sirens as first Cal came home, and then Einstein came home, and then right on the heels of Einstein . . . Riya came home.

Every single Camp Newton camper jumped from the bleachers and piled on top of Cal, Einstein, and Riya . . . including me and Sunny and Rachel.

Dr. Singh pulled Rachel off the pile, and she and Rachel climbed into the ambulance. "Molly's in charge," she instructed, but I saw her wink at Dr. Kassab, still sitting in the bleachers.

All of Camp Newton lined up on the dirt road and waved. Before they closed the ambulance doors, Dr. Singh blew Riya a kiss. And then she shouted, "Hey, Mathlings! Vegan tacos for everyone!"

"Hooah!" shouted Molly, and the rest of us cheered as the ambulance took off up the dirt road.

Once the ambulance was out of sight, we headed for the mess hall. Behind us, we heard the umpire yell, "BATTER UP!"

We looked at one another. "Oh my gosh. It's not over," Riya said. "There is still one more out to go."

There was some confusion, but then we got it. We needed one more batter. "Sunny Sweet," I yelled, and everyone joined in. "Sunny, Sunny, Sunny."

Sunny shrugged. Then she stuck on the helmet, picked up the bat, and wobbled out to home plate. When she got there, she looked up and gave me a little wave.

"PLAY BALL!" the umpire shouted, and Sunny lifted the bat off the ground just as the first strike flew past her.

"Come on, Sunny!" I called.

The next pitch hit the catcher's mitt with a dusty thud, and then Sunny swung.

"You can do it, Sunny!"

The catcher gave his sign. The pitcher wound up. Sunny crouched deep. The pitch whizzed toward Sunny, and she swung hard. And hit it! But only about three feet. She took off for first base, but the ball got there before she did by a mile.

"OUT!" shouted the first-base umpire. The game was over.

Once again, Camp Newton cheered. And then everyone began to chant, *"Ad infinitum, ad infinitum, ad infinitum."* Sunny took off the helmet and looked over at me. I pointed at her and mouthed the word "binary." Sunny giggled. And then I joined in on the chanting: *"Ad infinitum, ad infinitum, ad infinitum."*

The Falcon Hill campers stood in their bleachers watching us. One of them yelled out, "Hey, Camp Stupid. In case you didn't notice!" and then he pointed toward the scoreboard. Everyone on the softball field

looked to where he pointed. And there it was . . .
Falcon Hill 26, Newton 3.

Three. Not one. But three runs.

Camp Newton burst out into the loudest cheers
yet, and we kept it up all the way into the mess hall.

The Surprise

The word "surprise" is defined as "an unexpected or astonishing event, fact, or thing." I looked it up on my dictionary app. I'd been using the word "surprise" all my life, but it turns out that I didn't exactly know what it meant. When I thought of surprises I thought of balloons and presents and cakes and maybe horses . . . not unexpected or astonishing events.

My dad has a girlfriend.

That was an unexpected and astonishing event. So I guess it really was a surprise. And so there I was, all packed up and holding onto Sunny's hand and waiting for my dad's car to appear out of the pine trees. He texted us that he was a mile away, so Sunny and I hugged everybody good-bye and went outside to meet him . . . or rather, them.

We didn't tell anyone about the surprise. The morning was too happy. At breakfast, Dr. Singh had held a little ceremony where she gave each of us a trophy, even Molly. My trophy had my name on it and everything! And under my name it said COACH. I was going to put it on my dresser right in the middle, where I could see it from my bed. Everyone's trophy said something special. Junchao's said "Swimmer." Riya's said "MVP." Sam's said "Ambassador." Molly's said "Distinguished Service," and Sunny's said "Explorer." Sunny said it was her very favorite trophy ever. Mine was too, even if it was my only one.

I had my trophy in one hand and Sunny's hand in the other as I watched my father's car drive out of the pine trees and start down the hill to the camp. Dust followed behind it, and the sun shone off of the windshield. We listened to the faraway crunching of the tires on the dirt. And listened.

"It's taking him forever to get down this road," I whispered.

"It's been only twenty-eight seconds since his car came out of the trees," Sunny says. "I've been timing it."

I took my eyes off the car and looked down at Sunny. "Why?" I asked.

She took a breath, and I stopped her. "I don't want to know."

We smiled at each other and then turned back toward the car coming to a stop in front of us.

"Remember ShopRite," I whispered.

She squeezed my hand.

I squeezed hers back.

Dad parked next to Poly and then climbed out of the car. Sunny and I squinted up at him. He looked the same as he always did, only more tan. He swooped down on us and gave us a gigantic hug, squishing me and Sunny and our trophies together. "Girls, girls, girls," he said, his voice vibrating through me. It was the warmest, tightest, sweetest, nicest hug in the whole entire world, and it almost made me forget what was coming next . . . almost.

He let us go and leaned back. "Well?" he asked. "Ready?"

Sunny and I grabbed each other and stared at him. "Ready," I squeaked. And I felt Sunny's nails dig into my arm.

He picked up our two orange backpacks and walked them back to the trunk. I wanted to peek inside the car, but I was too scared. I didn't see any movement, so maybe she was waiting for Daddy to open her door.

He shut the trunk and walked around the car. "I thought you guys were ready?" he said.

Sunny and I looked at each other. And then we looked back at him. "What is it?" he asked. "Is something wrong?"

"We are," I said. "We're . . . waiting . . . for the, you know," I said.

He shook his head back and forth. My heart soared. Maybe it was a mistake. Maybe Sunny made a mistake.

"The surprise," said Sunny.

The sun went behind a cloud and I saw Dad get it, and I was reminded that once again . . . Sunny Sweet does not make mistakes.

"The surprise," he said, nodding. "And you both know what it is, don't you?"

We shook our heads yes.

"Well, girls," he said. "I did not bring the surprise."

It was as if Sunny and I had been holding up the universe for the past six minutes and now it had lifted off us and flown away. Daddy must have seen it fly away because he knelt right down by us and looked deep into our eyes. "We'll talk, okay? And you two can tell me all about camp and I'll tell you all about the surprise and everything will be okay. And," he added, "we'll do it over lunch. How do cheeseburgers and french fries sound?"

Like music to my ears. But I didn't say that. I just said that it sounded good. And Sunny said she'd have a veggie burger.

"You're a vegetarian?" asked my dad.

"Let's just go," I said.

We climbed into the car, and Dad told us to buckle up. Sunny pointed out that her seat belt used a clasping system and not a buckle system, and that a buckle system was typically a rectangular frame with a hinged pin and that a clasping system used a rotation path of insertion. She said some more stuff using words like joint and mechanism and interlocking, but I wasn't listening.

Dad swung the car around and headed out of Camp Newton. I looked back in time to see Sam and Riya walk out of the mess hall and head toward Dr. Singh's office. Sam was carrying Ronald in his box. He had adopted the grasshopper since Junchao had flown home this morning and she wasn't allowed to take him on the flight. I gave them a wave, but I knew they couldn't see me. I turned back around in my seat and thought about how fun next summer was going to be.

Dad looked at me in his rearview mirror and smiled.

"Dad?" I said.

"Yes, honey?"

"Can I have a horse?"

"No," he said.

I laughed. And then I grabbed my little sister—clasping system and all—and squeezed.

Sunny Sweet Is So NOT Scary

I'm in charge!" I said.

"Mom said Mrs. Song was in charge," said Sunny.

"Mrs. Song is in charge only in an emergency," I told her. "And watching a movie is not an emergency."

This was my very first sleepover and I didn't want my little sister hanging out with us the entire night. I was trying to pay more attention to Sunny since we got back from summer camp and I had already let her stay for crafting (Junchao, Alice, and I made friendship bracelets while Sunny strung DNA strands), karaoke (Sunny sang something she called a gregory chant that went on *forever*), Scrabble (Sunny won with "jonquils"), and painting our nails (Junchao chose purple, Alice chose black, I chose orange, and Sunny melted all our Styrofoam cups into the nail polish remover). It was time for this to be *my* first sleepover and not Sunny's.

"Good night, Sunny," I said.

Sunny hung her little head and walked out of the living room.

Once she was gone, Junchao broke down. "I feel bad for her, Masha. What about letting her stay for the movie?"

"Yeah," said Alice. "And then you can tell her to go to bed. Because you have to admit, the Styrofoam cup thing was kind of cool. What did she say happened? Something about pollywogs?"

"Polymers," said Junchao, "which are long chains of monomers."

"Guys," I said. "Forget Dr. Frankensunny. This sleepover is only for the *Xing Yun San You,* which is what Mrs. Song always called Alice, Junchao, and me. In English it means the *Lucky Three* because we were three great friends and the number three is lucky in Chinese culture. "Plus," I added. "It's a scary movie, and Sunny doesn't like scary movies."

This was totally true. Sunny didn't like scary movies. Not because she got scared, but because none of it was, "scientifically possible." The movies annoyed the skinny little genius. And the skinny little genius annoyed me while I was trying to watch them. She always wanted to talk about matter and molecules

when all I wanted to do was shout, *"Don't go down into the basement!"*

Alice, Junchao, and I huddled together on the couch with a big bowl of popcorn in front of us. I hugged my cuddly stuffed Eeyore that Alice got me from Disney World and clicked through our choices for the movie. I'd been looking forward to this night with my two best friends ever since I got home from summer camp.

The whole sleepover thing had actually been my mom's idea. She felt so bad about Sunny turning the dude ranch into Camp Newton, and about my surprise horse turning into my father's new girlfriend, Claudia, that she suggested I have my very first sleepover. But then after we planned everything, she was asked to attend a conference for work last minute.

It looked like the whole night was off, and I didn't know what was worse—that I wasn't having the sleepover or that I had to tell Alice that I wasn't having the sleepover. Alice flipped out just like I knew she would. She said that if I canceled the sleepover, her parents would probably never let her go to another one again because it had taken her a week to convince her mom and dad to let her go to this one. Her parents were mega nervous about Alice needing special stuff because of her spine problems from her spina bifida.

But then Mrs. Song saved the day. She said she'd help out with the sleepover and spend the night at our house. Mrs. Song had been a nurse back in China, and that made Alice's parents really happy.

"Okay," I said, "we can watch *Zombie Revolution*, *Creatures of the Mist*, *Soul Snatchers*, or *Dark Poltergeists*."

"I choose none of those," Junchao cried. "They sound too scary."

"That's the point," I giggled. But I secretly agreed with Junchao. These movies did sound too scary. But this was what you did at a sleepover. It was required.

Junchao yawned.

"No, no, you can't be tired," I yelled. "It's way too early. We have to stay up all night."

"All night?" asked Junchao. "As in, until my mom picks me up in the morning?"

"Yes, that's the entire point of a sleepover . . . to stay up," I told her.

"I've never done that before," she said. "I don't know if I can."

"Humans are able to stay awake for up to 264 hours, or approximately eleven days," came a voice from behind the armchair. "Although you will show signs of progressive, and possibly significant, deficits in higher mental processes as the duration of sleep deprivation increases." It was Sunny's voice.

"Sunny!" I yelled. "Get out!"

I heard her scamper back to her room.

"Come on, you guys. We can do this," I said.

"Then let's choose *Dark Poltergeists*," Alice suggested. "I heard it was super scary."

"That's the spirit," I laughed. "Get it? Spirit."

"We get it," laughed Alice.

"I don't get it," said Junchao.

"Anyway," I said, "being scared will definitely keep us up."

"That's because the brain's hypothalamus activates both the sympathetic nervous system and the adrenal-cortical system, which make you become tense and alert with an increase in your heart rate and blood pressure known as the fight-or-flight response."

"SUNNY!" I shouted. "I'm going to tell Mrs. Song."

Again I heard her feet patter back down the hall.

I wasn't really going to bother Mrs. Song. She was already the greatest person ever because she said yes to doing this *and* she'd made us dumplings! I promised myself that no matter what happened, I wasn't waking up Mrs. Song. She had gone to sleep in my mother's bedroom after karaoke.

We shut off all the lights except for the lamp next to the couch, and I started the movie. As the music began and the beginning credits came on, a little story ran on the screen saying that the events were based on a real incident that took place in New Bedford, New Jersey.

"That's not that far from here," Junchao breathed.

"Don't worry. We're all together," I said.

But I was worried. I didn't like that this was a true story and that it happened so close by. I took the blanket from the back of the couch and put it around us. Alice took Junchao's one hand and I took her other hand. Junchao smiled a little less worried-looking smile. It made me feel better, too, and the three of us got comfortable.

At first, the movie looked like it was just about a normal family that moves into a new house. But then strange things started to happen. Footsteps echoed down the hall at night. The lights flickered on and off for no reason. And the family heard a strange moaning coming from empty rooms in the house. Then a huge storm hit.

Lightning flashed across the screen. Thunder rumbled out of the television. All three of us jumped.

The boy from the family woke up, got out of bed, and walked slowly through the dark house—down a looooong hallway where an old clock stood *tick, tick, ticking* . . . past a shelf next to books where a doll sat with open, staring eyes . . . through a lonely dining room with lots of empty chairs . . . and then into the kitchen, where he switched on the light.

Junchao snatched the blanket away from us and threw it over her head.

"Nothing happened yet," I said.

"I'm getting ready," she answered, her voice muffled by the blanket.

Then the lights in the boy's kitchen went out, making Alice and me jump.

"What happened?" Junchao asked.

Before we could answer, the light next to our couch went out.

I looked at Alice. Alice's eyes glowed back at me. We dove under the blanket with Junchao.

"What happened? What happened?" asked Junchao.

"The light went out," Alice said.

"Did you see the ghost?" Junchao asked.

Alice gave a yelp, and the two of us practically crawled on top of Junchao at the idea that a ghost had turned off our light.

"*Our* light went out, Junchao. The one next to the couch," I whispered.

Junchao grabbed onto us. "There's a ghost in this house?" she screeched.

"Shhhh," I told her. I was afraid that if there was a ghost, it would hear her and then it would know that we knew that it was here.

We huddled under the blanket, listening to the storm still raging on the TV. I wondered why the ghost didn't turn that off too. Between two cracks of thunder I heard a tiny giggle.

I yanked the blanket off my head.

"Don't go out there," Junchao cried.

I cleared my throat and then in my best outdoor voice said, "Did you know that the pupils in your eyes constrict in the dark?" Mrs. Hull had taught us all about the human eye in science class last year. I knew that your pupils actually dilated, or grew bigger in the dark. They didn't constrict or get smaller. I also knew that *someone else* knew this.

"That's not true," said that *someone else*. "Your pupils dilate in the dark, allowing more light to enter the eye, improving your night vision."

Alice and Junchao threw off the blanket.

"Turn on the light, Sunny," I said.

There was silence for a second, and then Sunny said, "It's a ghoooooost." Her voice came from behind the window drape.

"It is not a ghost," I said. "It is a little sister who will be a ghost very soon if she does not turn on the light."

The light did not turn on.

"Sunny, come out from behind the drape," I said. "It's time for you to go to bed."

"Hoo, hoo, hoo."

"Sunny, that's the sound an owl makes . . . not a ghost!"

"Sunny is sleeeeepiiiiing; this is a ghoul-ie ghost.

I'm made up of pure energy, not ectoplasm, which isn't even real . . . like me."

I paused the movie, hopped off the couch, and turned the light back on. Then I walked to the window drape. When I swung it back, there stood Sunny.

"Boo?" she said, smiling.

"You are so *not* scary," I said.

Before Sunny could answer, the door to the basement rattled.

"Masha! Did you hear that?" asked Junchao.

Sunny danced out from behind the drape. "That was just the flow of gases caused by air moving from high pressure to low pressure. Sometimes it's called wind," she added.

"Did it just get cold in here?" Alice asked.

"Probably your veins under your skin are constricting to send more blood to major muscle groups as part of the fight-or-flight response, since you're scared about the door rattling. Less blood in your skin makes you cold."

There was a clomp, clomp, clomp of footsteps

coming from somewhere, but I couldn't tell exactly where.

"Mrs. Song?" I called. But somehow I knew that it wasn't Mrs. Song.

"Your veins are definitely constricting now," Sunny giggled.

"Shhh," I said. The four of us froze, listening . . . listening . . . listening. All was quiet.

Finally, Junchao sighed, Alice leaned back onto the couch, and I dropped into the armchair. It was nothing. I started to breathe again, and even though I tried not to think about it, I thought about the blood running back into my veins in my arms.

"Wooo."

We looked at Sunny. Sunny blinked back at us. She hadn't moved or said a word.

"Wooo. Woooo."

"What was that?" I asked.

All four of us dove under the blanket.

Acknowledgments

Thank you to Caroline Abbey for keeping me from Dublin. You are *always* right.

Thank you to Brett Wright for his patience with my poor pacing. You're the best . . . two days later . . . you're still the best!

Thank you to Kerry Sparks for being Kerry Sparks. No one else could handle that name.

And thank you to Linette Kim for being such a bright spot in the world.